WILDCAT OF THE SIERRA ESTRADA

A Yakima Henry Western

PETER BRANDVOLD

WOLFPACK
PUBLISHING
— EST 2013 —

WOLFPACK
PUBLISHING
— EST 2013 —

Paperback Edition
Copyright © 2021 (As Revised) Peter Brandvold

Published in the United States by Wolfpack Publishing, Las Vegas

Wolfpack Publishing
5130 S. Fort Apache Road, 215-380
Las Vegas, NV 89148

wolfpackpublishing.com

Paperback ISBN 978-1-64734-622-5
eBook ISBN 978-1-64734-621-8

WILDCAT OF THE
SIERRA ESTRADA

1

Bullets blew up dirt and gravel inches behind Yakima Henry's desperately running feet.

The half-breed ran hard, scissoring his arms and legs, his breath raking in and out of his lungs.

Rifles cracked and belched. Bullets ricocheted with wicked whines. One kissed the heel of Yakima's right boot. The two shooters fifty yards ahead of him whooped and hollered.

A boulder lay ten feet from Yakima. He bounded off the toes of his boots and was caroming through the hot, dry, desert air, hot lead screeching around him, when he saw the rattler idling in the shade behind the rock he was heading for with no way to change his course.

"Ahh, shitttttttt!"

The snake was slithering for a small hole opening along the base of the rock, but Yakima landed on the viper before it could poke its head into the hole. Yakima fought against his impulse to recoil, knowing that if he did, the serpent—a Mojave Green rattler, one of the deadliest snakes in the Southwestern desert—would likely pump him so full of poison, he'd bloat up like a javelina lying five days dead in a wash.

Instead, he pressed his chest and belly down hard against the snake, which he could feel writhing furiously beneath him, filling every nerve in the half-breed's tall, brawny body with instinctive revulsion.

At the same time, he could hear the two shooters running toward him, their boots grinding rocks and snapping cacti as they continued to whoop and holler and trigger lead in Yakima's direction. Several bullets screamed off the rock behind which Yakima lay flat, grinding his chest down hard against the panicking snake likely trying to twist its head around so it could sink its teeth through the man's buckskin tunic.

Yakima had once known a man who'd been bit in the chest by a rattler. His name had been Samuel Otter, and he'd been laying train rails with Yakima in western Kansas when he'd stepped away from the rail bed to take a piss, slipped on a rock, and fallen in some bushes. A sand rattler had sunk its fangs into his chest, just beneath his breastbone, filling his heart with black poison.

Otter had died screaming an hour later, clawing at his

chest as though to dig out the burning organ.

The shooters were closing on Yakima, shooting and yelling like coyotes on the blood scent. Soon, they'd have in their sites the half-breed, who was now the town marshal of Apache Springs, Arizona Territory. The bullets were getting closer. As the men's shadows began to slide toward Yakima's rock, the lawman shoved his hands under his chest and closed them around the piss-burned serpent's writhing body, one hand clenched just beneath the diamond-shaped head, the savage jaws open to expose the long, curved fangs.

The body curled up around itself and Yakima's gloved hands, the button tail arched and rattling shrilly.

Keeping his head down, Yakima took the snake in one hand and tossed it up and over the rock. The rattling increased as the snake plopped into the dirt. Suddenly, the shooting stopped.

One of the shooters yelled, "Snake, Goose!"

The warning hadn't entirely left the mouth of the first man, whose name Yakima knew was Curley Buck, a small-time criminal who'd robbed a whorehouse and cut a percentage girl the previous night in Apache Springs, before the other man, Buck's partner named Chuck "Goose" McGowan, gave a shrill, agonized cry.

"Oh, Jesus!" Curly Buck bellowed.

Goose gave another even shriller cry. A rifle belched.

Curley Buck loosed a strident scream.

Yakima grabbed his prized Winchester Yellowboy repeater, pumped a cartridge into the action, and pushed up onto his knees, swinging the Yellowboy's barrel over the top of his covering boulder. He held fire as Curley Buck, standing ten feet away and to Yakima's left, bellowed, "You done shot me, Goose!"

Curly Buck triggered his own Winchester at Goose McGowan, who stood another ten feet to the right of Buck, the viper hanging onto Goose's left leg, its fangs embedded in his thigh, near Goose's holstered six-gun. Goose was facing Curley Buck, whom he'd apparently inadvertently shot when the viper had struck.

Now Goose stumbled backward, dust rising around his spurred boots and billowing deerskin leggings, blood staining the right side of his collarless, pinstriped shirt.

"Fuck you, Curley!" Goose railed, lifting his carbine one-handed and sending another bullet—this one intentional—into the upper torso of his shorter, mustached partner, who already had one wound in his belly, just above his cartridge belt.

Curley Buck gave another enraged, agonized wail. He stumbled backward, nearly tripping over his own gravel-raking spurs, before pumping another cartridge into his Spencer repeater, snapping the butt plate to his shoulder, and hurling yet one more bullet into Goose, who gave his own bellowing cry in response.

He returned Curley Buck's fire.

All Yakima had to do was kneel there behind his boulder and watch in mute astonishment as the two raggedy-heeled, cork-headed criminals continued to exchange lead until they were both down and writhing, and the Mojave Green rattler was tracing a quick, serpentine route for the sanctuary of the high chaparral to the south.

"Well, I'll be damned," Yakima said, depressing his Yellowboy's hammer and lowering the Winchester to his side. "I didn't even have to burn any powder." He chuckled dryly to himself. "Can't beat that. Who said law-doggin' was hard?"

He'd taken the job of Apache Springs town marshal not long after the town had been burned by an especially nefarious criminal element, one with a very particular and deadly grudge against the entire town. The surviving members of the Apache Springs town council had beseeched Yakima to pin the badge to his shirt. Rather, the town council and the widow of the previous marshal—Julia Taggart.

In fact, that was the second time Julia Taggart had asked him to take the job, her dead husband's position. Both times Yakima had found himself accepting the offer, though he was as surprised as anyone who knew him would have been at his actually veering toward such permanent, reputable employment. Yakima Henry—a tall, slab-shouldered, jade-eyed German from his father's side, and a raw-boned, copper-toned, hawk-nosed Cheyenne from his mother's side—was not nor ever had been the law-dog sort.

In fact, anyone who knew him would have said he had more potential as an outlaw than a lawman. But Julia Taggart had had a hold on him.

She still did, sixteen months later.

Such a hold he hadn't felt the likes of since his beloved Faith had been killed by Bill Thornton up in Colorado, in fact.

A very strong hold, indeed. One that had him not remembering Faith quite so often these days. Or not as painfully. At least, he no longer woke from nightmares as regularly as before, screaming her name, his body bathed in sweat. It was nice to think about a living, breathing woman for a change. Also, sort of sad to finally be letting Faith go.

He did not think about this now, however, as he walked over to where Goose McGowan lay belly up, unmoving, in a patch of prickly pear. The recent events with the two criminals he'd tracked out of Apache Springs, and the deadly snake doing his job for him, still had him marveling at his uncustomary good luck.

Maybe the tide was changing for Yakima Henry. A

new job, a new woman, finally letting some grass grow beneath his feet...

The lawman stared down at Goose McGowan. The man's chest wasn't moving, and his eyes were half closed and glassy. He was a bloody mess, as were the cacti around and beneath him. The snake had chewed two gnarly-looking holes in his breeches, baring his bloody flesh that had already swollen up to half the size of Yakima's clenched fist.

Goose had cut his last whore.

Yakima crouched to dig around in the man's pockets, finding nothing more valuable than the twenty-five dollars in scrip and specie the son of a bitch had taken from Señora Galvez. "The Señora," as most knew her, owned and operated a locally famous parlor house in Apache Springs. The whorehouse, known simply as Señora Galvez's Place, was one of the first new establishments built after half of Apache Springs's business district had been turned to charred rubble by Rebel Wilkes, the ex-mining engineer who'd condemned the town and all its inhabitants.

Wilkes was dead now, and, with several pockets of high-quality, gold-bearing quartz having recently been found in the mountains around Apache Springs, the town had been rebuilt with almost dizzying speed.

In the year and a half since it had met its unceremonious near-demise, Apache Springs had almost doubled its previous size and was quickly growing larger. In fact, the spur line that Wilkes had gone into such a tizzy over not being able to construct himself was now being built by a Texas speculator named James Osgood, who'd convinced Apache Springs's new town council to turn over construction rights for a twenty-percent share of the new railroad's profits, of which he assured the six-man team of boosters there would be many more, what with all the bullion that would be shipped out of the Sierra Estrada—not to mention people pouring in to search for their own El Dorados—in the coming years.

Yakima pocketed the money he'd found on Goose. Señora Galvez would be happy to get it back, though what Goose and Curley had taken from the gold lockbox she kept in her boudoir wouldn't put much of a dent in the Mexican madam's considerable coffers. Yakima rarely saw the large, Victorian-like structure without a fairly steady stream of men issuing in or out, day or night. Señora Galvez kept the red lamp burning in her window twenty-four hours a day—unless one of her girls was giving birth, that is.

On that rare, problematic but understandable occasion, given the nature of the business, the light went out, and the drapes were drawn across the windows. Yakima suspected the shrewd, business-minded Señora didn't want to appall her clientele with the sounds of a wailing newborn, even though the child had likely been fathered by one of them.

Quickly, the child would be shunted off to an adoption agency in Phoenix or Denver, and the red light would burn with brash seediness once again...

Yakima found the rest of the stolen money in Curley Buck's shirt pocket. The twelve dollars he found there was blood speckled and slightly bullet torn, but Señora Galvez would be glad to see it just the same. She'd been in Apache Springs only a few months, but already her parsimony was legendary.

With the stolen money stowed safely in his right boot well, the lawman strode off in search of the robbers' two horses, which had run away during the gunfire. He found them grazing mesquite beans in a gully not far from where the bodies lay, already attracting flies. He whistled for his own horse, and the blaze-faced black stallion galloped in from where Yakima had left him well down the rise when he'd spied Curley and Goose stopping to rest and water their own horses, likely on their way to New Mexico.

They'd been savvier than Yakima had figured, and, spying the lawman on their back trail, they'd opened fire.

Yakima's mountain-bred stallion, Wolf, stopped a good ways off from where its rider was tying Goose belly down

13

across the dead man's saddle. The high-blooded stallion rippled his withers and shook his head so hard, he nearly threw off his bridle. Wolf didn't like the smell of blood any more than he liked the sound of gunfire, and he wasn't sure what to think about the dead men's two horses, both geldings who eyed him warily.

"Stand down, hoss," Yakima told the stallion. "Let's all be friends, all right? That way we'll get to town all the faster with no one's feelings getting hurt. I know you could do with a feed sack, and I sure as hell know I could do with one of Dundee's ales over to the Busted Flush."

Cleve Dundee had rebuilt his saloon in grand style after losing his original place in the fire. Losing his place and his left eye, that is, when Rebel Wilkes's human coyotes had run roughshod over the town. Dundee's establishment sat next to Señora Galvez's place and shared much of the same clientele.

Yakima thought the one-eyed saloon owner and madam might be sharing more than just clientele. Rumor had it that Dundee had been seen leaving the aging but well-preserved Spanish madam's private boudoir. Once, when making his rounds late at night, the half-breed lawman himself had spied Dundee slipping covertly down the whorehouse's back stairs from the third story, adjusting his eye patch and whistling a happy tune.

With his passing, the night air had been so liberally

scented with perfume and lilac water, Yakima had stifled a choking cough.

Now he finished tying Curly Buck over his claybank's back, lashing the dead man's tied ankles to his tied wrists beneath the mount's belly, then walked over and untied his own bridle reins from his saddle horn. He swung up onto Wolf's back, scrubbed sweat from his forehead with a sleeve of his buckskin shirt, and took a quick look around, getting his bearings.

Or trying to.

All around was rocky chaparral spiked with cactus. Red mesas and long, spine-like dykes rose in all directions, brightly reflecting the harsh sunlight of the high desert mid-afternoon. Coves of boulder-strewn earth and dinosaur teeth of jutting slabs of granite, limestone, and fire-blackened lava made this eastern leg of the Sierra Estrada a geologic maze. Yakima had been so intent on his quarry's sign that he wasn't sure what route he'd taken to get where he was.

Did his route back to town lie between those two tabletop mesas off to the northeast, or between the slant-topped mesa and jog of low sandy hills off to the northwest? He could backtrack himself, but that would take a while, given that the ground he'd followed the two robbers across was of long stretches solid volcanic rock blown up eons ago from cones jutting in the far west.

15

The half-breed almost randomly chose a route in the general direction of Apache Springs and booted Wolf into motion, trailing the two packhorses by their bridle reins.

An hour later, he felt a nettling unease. Chill fingers tapped across the back of his sweaty neck, and his innards squirmed like snakes.

He was lost.

He was also being followed.

2

Wolf had alerted him to the possible danger, as the horse, even more attuned to trouble than his rider, often did. The stallion had suddenly lifted his head and whickered deep in his chest, casting one brief glance over his shoulder.

Yakima had turned then, as well, and caught a glimpse of a horse and rider descending a steep grade maybe a hundred yards behind him. Horse and rider were a small, light-brown blur against the gray rock behind them, and then, as fast as Yakima had spied them, his shadower was gone, riding on down the grade and out of sight behind the boulders that fairly choked this canyon he'd found himself riding through, following the faint trace of an ancient Indian trail.

Yakima glanced behind him again now. Nothing. Just rocks of all shapes and sizes.

He turned his head forward, nudged the .44 residing

in its holster thonged to his right thigh, and loosened the Yellowboy in its scabbard jutting over his right stirrup fender. He looked around at the canyon whose northern wall, on his right, had grown taller the farther he'd ridden along its base. It must have been two hundred feet high in places—flues and chutes and crenellated, castle-like walls of eroded sandstone. There was virtually no growth except a few patches of wiry brown brush and cat claw, maybe a greasewood tuft or two.

To the south, on Yakima's left, was a massive jumble of boulders that had likely tumbled down from the northern ridge. That ridge, if comprised of all the rock that now nearly squeezed off Yakima's passage in places, must have been as tall as the northern ridge at one time. But something, maybe an earthquake, had caused that wall to collapse into the canyon.

Yakima knew he hadn't come this way. But maybe he'd find a western exit to the canyon. Apache Springs was north and west, and it really didn't matter which way he took to get there.

He cast a cautious glance behind him again. Not seeing his shadower, he kept riding.

The canyon turned this way and that, ever so gradually.

The hot sun's rays were relieved by long shadows angling out from the northwestern wall.

Yakima followed another curve in the wall to his right,

turning back toward the north, and abruptly jerked back on Wolf's reins. The horse whickered uneasily, blew. Staring at something on the ground a ways ahead and near the base of the northern wall, Yakima put the horse a little farther ahead, then stopped him again.

He stared down at what remained of a man who'd been staked out spread-eagle on the canyon floor. Little more than a mere skeleton. There were three men, in fact. Two more skeletons lay just beyond the first one.

The half-breed stared at the nearest man—sun-bleached bones to which a few bits of sun-mummified skin and scraps of clothing clung. A few sparse patches of skin also clung to the skull, and hair clung in similar patches to the scalp. The bony wrists were lashed with dried scraps of rawhide to stakes that had been driven into the ground.

Yakima put Wolf a little farther ahead, scrutinizing the other two skeletons, which were in similar shape as the first. He shifted his attention to the sandstone wall beyond them, into which someone had scratched *TURN BACK OR DIE* in both English and Spanish: *ROCEDEN O MORIR.*

Yakima glanced about, feeling those cool fingers of apprehension once more. He hipped around to peer along his back trail. No sign of his shadower, if the rider back there had been shadowing him. Maybe two people out here in this dinosaur mouth of geologic chaos had merely been a coincidence, and the rider had gone his own way.

Lord knew this devil's playground was home to more than a few prospecting desert rats from both north and south of the border.

Or maybe the rider was the person who'd scribbled the bilingual warning into the canyon wall. Maybe the jake had a mining claim nearby, and the three poor devils lying stretched out on the red caliche of the canyon floor, like sacrifices to Father Sun, had been claim jumpers.

"Don't get nervy, pard," Yakima said to no one in particular as he booted Wolf on down the canyon, running his wary gaze across the rubble strewn to his left and from which a bushwhacker would find plenty of hiding places. "I ain't out to crowd anyone off their diggin'. Just tryin' to find a route back to Apache Springs, that's all. Back to the Springs and a tall, cool, malty ale in the Busted Flush..."

He fairly groaned at the imagined malty wetness of Dundee's personally brewed ale, from malted barley he shipped in from Kansas via the Southern Pacific and a regular train of freight wagons. The two packhorses clomped along behind Yakima, shod hooves occasionally ringing off cracked stones. The three dead men of bones fell back over his right shoulder.

Yakima rounded the bend in the trail and stopped once more. He stared into a broad, flat area opening to his right. Ahead, near the base of the canyon wall looming far above, sat a small, box-like adobe structure that looked almost toy sized in contrast to the cliff towering over it. A belfry had been mounted over the apparently doorless front entrance set atop crumbling stone steps.

A church? Way out here?

Yakima nudged Wolf forward, particularly interested in what appeared to be a well sitting in front of the church, within a circular wall of stone coping and shaded by a small brush *ramada*. He was low on water, and the longer he spent out here, he would naturally get lower. He had three horses to water in addition to himself, and Curley and Goose's own canteens were only about one-third full of the warm, brackish substance.

He drew up in the yard of the church, stopped Wolf and the packhorses over which his dead quarry slouched, and looked around once more. Turning to the church, he called, "Hello!"

A slight pause while he watched, listened. "Anyone here?"

His voice sounded inordinately loud, echoing in the canyon's crypt-like silence.

He stared at the church and the flat, hard-packed canyon floor around it. There appeared to be no one here. Judging by the lack of prints in the thin, red soil stippled here and there by chips of red gravel, no one

21

had been here in a while. A gust of a hot breeze rose from behind him, kicked up a curtain of tan dust, blew it over Yakima and the horses, and set it ticking against the side of the church slumped before him like a derelict boat, if boats could be made of cracked, water-stained, sun-bleached adobe.

Yakima's long, sweat-damp black hair rose, dancing across his face. He lifted his low-crowned, flat-brimmed, black hat with one hand and pulled his hair back behind his head with the other. He ran a buckskin sleeve across his face again, swabbing the sweat, then set his hat back down.

The breeze was hot and dusty. Still, a cold thread ran through it. Cold as air blowing across a frozen lake in the North Country.

No. Couldn't be.

The chill he felt came from inside. There was something dark and cold about this canyon. Something that continued to make writhing snakes of his innards and squeeze his heart in a dark fist of doom. It was a foreboding of... what?

Evil.

Still, he felt oddly compelled to investigate. Why not? The horses needed water and a rest.

He turned Wolf around and rode over to the well. He swung down from the saddle and peered over the well coping, spying the oily glint of water about ten feet down.

An old bucket sat on the edge of the coping, attached to a wooden winch with a frayed rope. He dropped the bucket into the well, winched it back up, the winch working hesitatingly, spindly with age, and then poured water from the bucket into his hat. He set the hat on the ground before Wolf, then set the bucket on the ground before the two dead men's horses.

The claybank began drinking first while the second horse, a dapple gray, drooped its head and flicked its ears, waiting patiently for its own turn.

Yakima had enough of the old frontiersman in him to allow his horse to drink before he himself did. After all, without a horse—especially out here in this godforsaken desert—a man wouldn't last long.

Patting the black's rump, he told the horse to stay there and then, looking cautiously around once more, feeling a cold thumb of apprehension pressing taut against the base of his spine, he began striding toward the church. As he walked, the breeze continued to gust. He flicked the keeper thong free from over the hammer of his .44 and then mounted the stone steps, treading lightly and carefully, for the mortar between the stones was loose.

The steps had to be a couple of hundred years old.

He stopped at the top of the steps and peered

through the broad open door. The door itself, or what was left of it, lay on the floor to Yakima's right—little more than moldering bits of rotten wood. Cobwebs had taken its place, the webs stitched with dead flies, dead leaves, and dust.

Yakima parted the sticky web with his arm and stepped through the doorway to stop just inside. Nothing here but dirt and other debris littering the floor, blown in through several glassless windows in the stout walls to the left and right. The smell of bat guano and mouse shit. Glancing to his right, Yakima saw a partly devoured rabbit carcass, probably left there by some coyote that had entered the ancient church to dine and maybe spend a recent evening. More, similar bones lay strewn amongst the rubble.

Another breeze gust sent more dust through the windows to Yakima's right. Squinting against it, he stared at what appeared to be an altar at the far front of the church. Atop the altar sat a large crate or box of some sort, which shone in a thick ray of golden sunlight spilling into the church from a window to its left. Slowly but steadily he moved down the center of the church, between two rows of crumbling wooden benches where worshipers had apparently sat—how long ago?

He stopped before the altar. The box was a trunk— roughly the size of a large steamer trunk. There was no lock, no padlock or chain. The box sat coated in dust and cobwebs atop the cracked adobe altar.

Yakima's heart quickened inexplicably as he placed both of his gloved hands on the sides of the lid and opened it. Dry steel hinges squawked. The lid shifted precariously in the half-breed's hands. Sunlight angling down from the left began to smolder and glisten as the lid rose and fell back away to rest atop the altar on the other side of the trunk.

There appeared a veritable fire inside the trunk. The flames were so bright that Yakima had to look away briefly, then squint.

No, not fire. Sunlight glistened off what appeared to be pure gold trinkets heaped inside the trunk.

Yakima's heart danced, and his legs weakened. His breath became short and strained, like an old man's.

"Holy…"

The trinkets were mounded to the top of the box. He plucked up one and scrutinized it—a gold griffin with tiny, demonic eyes and bared fangs. Yakima set the griffin aside and picked up what appeared to be a winged angel with the face of a small child. Like the griffin, it was roughly the same size as his clenched fist.

Setting the angel aside, he picked up another angel and then a cherub and then a crucifix and then a gold, jewel-encrusted ring. Then a jewel-encrusted bracelet.

There were many coins of all sizes and bearing Latin crosses. There were necklaces and miniature daggers and molded depictions of what Yakima, not a religious man, figured were saints.

He continued to rummage through the box of solid gold doodads until his face was bathed in sweat and his heart was hammering his breastbone. He'd never had such a feeling before. He'd never figured himself suscep-tible to such gold fever.

But, then, what man would not have such a reaction when confronted with so much wealth? He had no idea what the contents of the trunk were worth, but he figured likely in the millions of dollars.

"Holy... shit," he muttered.

He drew a deep breath and stepped back away from the trunk.

Words of his friend the Rio Grande Kid, also known as the outlaw Johnny Day, who now worked as Yakima's deputy town marshal in Apache Springs, spoke to him with remembered quiet eagerness, with a weird, almost lewd intimacy that untold wealth often inspires in men who rarely had more than a few cents to their names at any one time:

"...when Eddie was comin' up through the Estrada, he stumbled on an old abandoned mine and a Mexican church in a deep canyon. There was gold everywhere...

and what looked to Eddie like a treasure box from some Spanish galleon. Spilling over with jewels of every shape, size, and color. And you know what else Eddie found in that canyon?... Eddie found a cannon made of pure gold!"

The words seemed to have been spoken out loud in the church and were now echoing off the walls.

The walls.

Yakima had vaguely noticed something odd about them.

There was gold everywhere!

Frowning, Yakima stepped around behind the altar. He moved up to the back wall, shoved his face up to within a few inches to study it closely.

It appeared to have been tiled. The tiles were dark, mostly in rectangular shapes roughly twelve inches long by three inches wide. At first, Yakima thought the tiles were some kind of stone, but he'd never seen stones that off-gray, almost copper color.

His heart once again beginning to race. He dipped a hand into a pocket of his denim trousers and pulled out a coin. He shoved his hand forward and scraped the quarter against one of the tiles, plowing up nearly a quarter-inch crust of dust and grime of many years, laying bare a small strip of pure, glistening gold.

Gold so bright that, with the sun from a near window reflecting off of it, it was like a miniature dagger poking his eyes!

Yakima stepped back, his heart thudding slower now but with more vigor against his sternum. He turned to the right wall. It was tiled in the same stuff. He swung around, breathless, to face the left wall.

Same stuff.

He tipped his head far back on his shoulders to study the ceiling eight feet above his head.

Sure enough. Same stuff.

The walls and ceiling of this church lost in a deep, rubble-strewn chasm were tiled in pure gold ingots!

Not only that, but...

Something crouched low against the wall to his right, partly concealed in the wall's heavy shadows. Yakima knelt beside it, laid a hand against the side of a long, tapering barrel. The barrel of a cannon whose wooden wheels were nearly disintegrated. It slumped nearly sideways against the gold wall.

Again, he used the coin to scrape away the grit, revealing another line of pure gold.

The gold cannon from Eddie's treasure tale!

Yakima straightened, stumbled backward, throbbing heart swelling in his chest. He stared up at the ceiling. He didn't realize it, but his mouth was hanging nearly wide open as he continued to study the ceiling as though in a trance.

He closed it when he heard the soft ring of what sounded like a spur outside the front door.

He lowered his head in time to see a man in a long, black duster and brown Stetson standing silhouetted against the outside light, aiming a pistol straight out from his right shoulder.

Flames and smoke lapped from the barrel.

3

Yakima threw himself to his left as the shooter's bullet screeched over his right shoulder to bark against the gold-paneled wall behind him.

He hit the floor—which he just then realized was also tiled in gold!—and rolled off his left shoulder as the shooter flung more lead, the next bullet spanging off the floor two feet in front of him, the ricochet burning a fine line across his cheek. He rolled again... and again, dodging another bullet... and on the next roll he came up on his heels and propelled himself nearly straight up and out the low, rectangular window in the church's east wall.

The shooter's pistol thundered hollowly inside the church, on the heels of another bullet slicing through the air over Yakima's head as he hit the ground outside with a grunt and rolled onto his back. His ears rang, and his cheek burned.

"Goddamnit!" yelled a voice near the front of the church.

Spurs chinked angrily.

Yakima slipped his stag-horned .44 from its holster as he rolled up onto his haunches. He clicked the hammer back and extended the pistol straight out from his right shoulder as the shooter strode quickly around the church's front corner.

The Colt bucked and roared in Yakima's hand.

The shooter had just cleared the corner and turned to face him, bringing her gun around—*yeah, a girl*—and now she screamed as the half-breed's bullet chewed into her right arm. She dropped her own smoking Colt and flew backward in the dust, her hat tumbling off her head, and her flaxen hair spilling in thick curls about her shoulders.

Quickly, Yakima gained his feet. "Emma?"

She turned to him, throwing her hair back behind her head, clamping her left hand over her upper right arm. Her hazel eyes were cast with pain and surprise. "*Yakima? What… what are you doing out here?*"

The half-breed holstered his Colt and dropped to a knee beside her. "I was about to ask you the same thing." He pulled her hand away from her arm. "How bad you hit?"

"I don't know, but it hurts like a devil! Thanks a bunch, *Marshal!*"

"You're lucky I didn't blow your head off. That's what I was aiming for!" Yakima pulled the ragged edges of her bullet-torn duster and checked shirt back away from the wound.

"Ouch!" she cried.

"Hell," he said, giving a wry snort. "I've stubbed my toe worse than that gettin' up at night to evacuate my bladder."

"I bet you don't use such farm talk as that around my uppity sister." Emma Kosgrove's voice was pitched with accusation. She was the younger sister of Julia Taggart, the former town marshal's widow Yakima had taken more than a little fondness to in Apache Springs.

Yakima had met Emma before he'd met Julia, who, at twenty-four, was older than Emma by five years. He'd met Emma out in the desert nearly two years ago, when he'd first come to this country with a mining claim he'd won in a poker game. He and Emma had both been hunting, and he'd shot the black-tailed deer she'd been aiming at. She rode her buckskin over, fighting mad and sassy as hell, the way rich, privileged girls could be. Her father, originally from the east, owned the Conquistador gold mine. Emma had piped down when Yakima had silently field-dressed the deer and thrown it over the back of her horse.

"What're you doing?" she'd said, startled, as he shoved his Arkansas toothpick back into the sheath behind his neck.

"I figure one bullet and one deer is a small price to pay for a little peace and quiet."

With that, he'd swung up onto Wolf's back and ridden off to find another deer for his cellar.

He didn't know if she'd followed him home that day or just figured he must be occupying the old stone cabin in the Javelina Bluffs, but she showed up there two days later. She'd showed up unexpectedly several times after that—a hot-blooded, flaxen-haired, hazel-eyed beauty, her tan, marble-smooth right cheek bearing a single mole that gave an exotic definition to her face.

She and Yakima had become lovers for a time, though that was over now. At least, as far as he was concerned. Eventually he'd learned that she'd joined her father at the Conquistador several years ago, when her mother had died in Boston and she'd been expelled from her girl's school for failing grades and general delinquency.

Learning that, he'd softened toward her. They shared a bond of sorts. The bond of the black sheep, though he, being a half-breed in a white man's world, was decidedly blacker and not half as pretty. He'd come to call her the Wildcat of the Sierra Estrada, because in many ways she was every bit as wild as the pumas and bobcats that stalked these mountains, always hunting...

Maybe she was as lonely, too, her father being more interested in finding more gold than spending time with

Emma. That's why she could nearly always be found on her fine-boned buckskin, riding these mountains, looking for something, though Yakima doubted even Emma knew what...

But then, remembering what he'd found in the church, maybe he did know what she'd been looking for... and found.

As he plucked his red handkerchief from his back pocket and wrapped it around the girl's arm, he frowned at her suspiciously. "Let's leave your sister out of this," he said and narrowed one eye. "What're you doing out here, shooting first and asking questions later? Though the way you flung lead at me just now, I doubt you were hoping there'd be anyone alive later to ask any questions."

She winced as he drew the hanky's knot tight, then glanced at him incredulously. "You saw, I take it? What's inside?"

"I sure as hell did. How did you know about it? We must be a good twenty miles from the Conquistador." She lived in a sprawling house near the remote gold mine with her father and a full-blood Chiricahua butler, Three Moons.

"You're all turned around," Emma snorted, tossing her hair again as she jerked her chin west. "The Conquistador is only five miles as the crow flies... and as I ride," she added snootily, "that way. Apache Springs is straight

34

north, a dozen miles or so."

"Well, shit," Yakima said, raking a sheepish thumb down his unshaven jaw and rising to his feet. "I did get turned around."

"Who're they?" Emma asked as Yakima pulled her to her feet. She glanced at the two dead men lying belly down across their horses standing by the well with Wolf.

The stallion hadn't alerted Yakima of the girl's approach because he'd known her and the buckskin that now stood nearby, reins dangling. Wolf had assumed, albeit wrongly, that Emma Kosgrove hadn't been out to trim his rider's wick, the half-breed silently opined, brushing his hand across the bullet burn on the nub of his left cheek.

"Those two fellas cut a whore and robbed Señora Galvez in Apache Springs," he said.

"You brought 'em down, I take it."

Yakima chuckled darkly. "They took themselves down with a little help from a Mojave Green sidewinder."

Emma scowled at him. "A *what?*"

"Never mind." Yakima walked over to the front of the church, mounted the steps, and stood peering inside once more, still not sure that he'd really seen what he thought he'd seen before he'd been so rudely interrupted. "How long have you known about this place, Emma?"

He moved inside, and she walked up behind him.

35

Immediately, he had that feeling again. The jitters. Gold fever.

It was as though the walls were filled with shimmering lightning, and the fires were oozing through his bones, causing his hands and feet to tingle, his nerves to dance. He still couldn't wrap his mind around how much wealth was here, lining the walls of this small, derelict hovel out here in this likely uncharted, unmapped canyon.

No. It wasn't unmapped. Eddie had mapped it and, dying when a posse had ridden him down and shot him, had turned the map over to his friend, the Rio Grande Kid. The Kid still had the map. In fact, on his days off, the Kid often wandered out here with his map, looking for this very canyon.

The gold fever burned through the half-breed's veins. At the same time, a chill lingered at the back of his neck. That presentiment of evil he'd felt before discovering the gold...

"I've known for about three years," Emma said. "That's when I rode in here by accident, heading west. I reckon that's how you did it, too."

"I was heading back to Apache Springs, lost my trail."

Their boots crunched the dead leaves and gravel and other debris littering the church's gold floor—beneath the debris and several layers of desert grime. The half-breed lawman was thinking about the Rio Grande Kid and his treasure map. *My, won't the Kid be surprised to learn just how much treasure was really here?*

"Yakima?"

He turned to the girl again, raking his gaze from the gold-tiled wall to his left. Emma gazed at him gravely, her eyes filled with a deep desperation. "What is it?" He walked over to her, took her hand, and lifted her arm so he could inspect his handkerchief. "You bleeding?"

She pulled her hand away and continued to stare up at him with a strange anguish. Slowly, she shook her head. "Yakima, no one must know about this canyon. The church. Any of it."

He stared back at her, waiting for her to continue.

"I promised old Jesus that I would make sure no one knew about it. At least… I promised to do my best."

"I don't get it. Who's Jesus?" Yakima paused, absorbing the information. "Don't tell me you killed those three men staked out—"

Shaking her head, Emma cut him off. "Jesus did. They were outlaws on the run from Mexico. They stumbled into this canyon like I did… like you did… and started to fill their saddlebags from the gold in the box. They probably would have come back for the rest… maybe brought others… and…"

"Jesus killed them?"

"He had to."

"Why? Who was this Jesus fella—some prospector who stumbled upon this canyon and wanted it all for himself?"

Emma shook her head, frowning. "No. It wasn't like that. It's *not* like that!"

"What do you mean it's *not* like that? Where's Jesus?"

"Dead."

"Who killed him?"

"Rattlesnake crawled into his bed one night for warmth, and Jesus rolled over on it. I found him two days later, near death."

Yakima winced, involuntarily feeling the Mojave Green rattler squirming against his own chest...

Emma opened her mouth to continue, but then distant thunder rumbled, and she turned to the west windows. Clouds were scudding across the ground outside the church. She placed a hand on Yakima's arm. "I'll explain later. Let's stable our horses."

"Where?"

Emma strode to the open door. "I'll show you." She stopped and, seeing the big, green-eyed lawman just standing there, gazing at her skeptically from beneath his flat-brimmed, black hat, said, "No more questions for now. I'll explain everything later, once we're in out of the rain."

"In out of the rain where?"

She smiled and gave a coquettish wink. "My secret place."

She flounced out into the yard, buttocks pushing against the worn seat of her gray denim trousers as the black duster blew out behind her. Yakima looked away quickly, not liking the tug the image of her heart-shaped rump gave his loins.

***

.

Yakima fired a lucifer to life on the buckle of his cartridge belt.

He touched the flame to the end of the quirley he'd just rolled and drew the smoke deep into his lungs, staring at the rain hammering nearly straight down and forming a billowing white curtain over the desert around him.

He stood on the narrow front gallery of Emma's "secret place"—an ancient, two-room adobe shack with a beehive fireplace, a small eating table, a few chairs—one made of wicker and padded with straw-stuffed deerskin—and a large cot whose legs were formed of crisscrossed iron-wood trunks. Its straw-stuffed ticking mattress was covered with threadbare sheets, an equally threadbare quilt, and two sewn-together mountain lion hides. The desert nights got cold, even colder now in the late fall.

Javelina skins acted as throw rugs on the shack's hard-packed earthen floor, which was the color of iron heated to glowing in a blacksmith's forge.

There were rudimentary shelves and a wooden dry sink and rickety washstand with a rusty tin washbowl perched on top, with a cracked mirror secured to the ceiling beam above, beside a deer antler comb hanging from another nail. Yakima could hear Emma in there now, filling a pan for coffee from a wooden water bucket.

As Yakima smoked, he slid his gaze to the right of the old shack to where Wolf and the two dead men's horses and Emma's buckskin stood beneath a brush *ramada* in a small, stone corral, the corral's fence and gate constructed from woven mesquite and cedar branches. The horses stood still as statues, lined up side by side, watching the rain tumble off the *ramada* into the dirt of the ancient corral.

The cabin and corral were tucked into a notch in the canyon wall, screened from the church by boulders that had tumbled into the canyon when the southern ridge had collapsed. Yakima wouldn't have known the hovel was here unless the Wildcat of the Sierra Estrada had shown him—just in time to avoid the late-summer monsoon downpour, in fact. They'd just finished tending the horses, and Yakima had just finished laying out Goose and Curley Buck behind the lean-to stable attached to the corral, when the skies had opened up.

Wildcat of the Sierra Estrada...

Yakima hadn't realized how appropriate the name

he'd dubbed the girl had been. She'd been living out here only a handful of years, but she must have known every nook and cranny of this remote range, a spur range of the Chiricahuas. She probably knew every gold-seeking desert rat within a hundred square miles and had shared a pan of coffee and pot of beans with him more than once.

The lonely, adventurous sort. Beautiful, too.

Get your mind off her damned ass, you cur.

"What's the matter?" she said now, giving him a mild start as she stepped through the doorway behind him. Her voice had been soft and melodic beneath the steady din of the rain.

"Huh?"

Emma stopped beside him, holding two smoking tin coffee cups. "You were snorting and shaking your head."

"Oh, nothin'."

"Nothin', huh?" Emma curled one side of her mouth as she held up one of the cups.

Yakima's ear tips warmed.

She sipped her coffee and stared out at the storm. "Were you remembering?" she asked him, smiling up at him again, her hazel eyes bright with teasing.

Yakima frowned as he blew on the coal-black, steaming surface of his coffee. "I wasn't remembering a damn thing. I was thinking about this canyon... that church... the wealth here. All of it."

41

"I can see by the flush in your cheeks you were think-ing about more than the wealth here. Er... at least, not just the gold wealth here."

"Be quiet, Emma."

"So you were!"

"What?" he said angrily, his ears fairly burning now.

"You were remembering our first time. You know—the first time we made *love*?" She flounced close beside him. "At your old shack in the Javelina Bluffs. In the rain..."

How could he help remembering the vision of her stripping off her clothes and dancing naked in the desert downpour? A vixeny desert sprite. A blonde-headed, ripe-breasted, round-hipped succubus of the Sierra Estrada. He'd joined her naked in the yard, and they'd danced together—if you could call it dancing. He'd lifted her onto the edge of the well and taken her like a love-hungry stallion.

He could still hear her love cries echoing in his head.

He tried hard to listen to the rain, wanting the storm to drive the echoes out.

It wasn't her he'd set his hat for. Not that he'd set his hat for anyone. But, if he had, that person would be her sister, Julia. Not as sexual, maybe. Not as wild. But every bit as beautiful. Besides, he felt a kinship with the older daughter of Hugh Kosgrove, for Julia had lost someone as important to her as he had.

She knew how he felt; he knew how she felt.

Emma set her cup on the gallery rail, walked up to Yakima, placed her hands on his chest. She smiled lustily up at him, began to slide her face toward his. He stared at her mouth, the fullness of her lips, and couldn't help seeing them together in the Javelina Bluffs.

He drew his head back. "Forget it."

"You know you don't mean that," she said, wrapping her arms around his neck, trying to pull his head down to hers.

"Forget it. I want to talk about this canyon."

Suddenly, Emma's eyes hardened. She removed her arms from around his neck and turned her mouth corners down. "Are you going to deny yourself *me* because of Julia?"

"I know how you feel about her, Emma... about your own sister. There's no point in talking about it. So, take your coffee, sit down, and tell me about this treasure-laden canyon and your friend Jesus."

4

"No," Emma said, taking her coffee cup in her hands and leaning back against the gallery rail, the pouring rain flanking her. "I won't tell you a thing about this canyon. I won't tell anyone. I promised Jesus I wouldn't, just as he promised the others who came before him."

She turned her head sharply, defiantly, to one side to stare off toward the unseen, gold-laden church.

"Others?" Yakima said. "You mean there were others before Jesus? Other"—he looked around as though for the right word—"*protectors* of the canyon?"

Emma stared at him, holding her cup in both hands just under her chin. "Tell me about Julia, Yakima. What rare trait does my sister have that makes it so easy for her to steal men away from me?"

Anger burned in him. "Men? There was only one you could say she 'stole' from you, Emma. That was Lon. And it wasn't something she'd wanted to do. She didn't set out to hurt you. It just worked out that way. She and Lon felt something… something *lasting*… between each other. And it would have lasted, too…"

He walked up to the rail several feet away from Emma and stared moodily out at the rain. "It would have lasted if she hadn't been taken from me." He caught himself suddenly and turned to Emma quickly. "I meant—it would have lasted if Taggart hadn't been taken from her. Killed by Rebel Wilkes."

He sipped his coffee to cover his chagrin.

Wilkes, who'd worked as chief mining engineer for Emma's father, had been the first man Julia had been slated to marry. But then he'd gone off on his own and staked his own gold claim, and that had set him at odds with Julia's and Emma's father, Hugh Kosgrove, who'd founded the Conquistador. So Kosgrove had banished Wilkes and made Julia break off the engagement.

"So that's it."

Yakima was staring out at the rain again. He turned sharply, a little surprised to see that Emma had sidled soundlessly up to him. She stared up at him from just below his left shoulder. "That's what you see in her. Her grief." Kosgrove's younger daughter shook her head darkly. "Grief isn't much of a bedrock to lay the foundation of a marriage on."

Yakima snorted. "Who said anything about marriage?"

"You have that look in your eyes. I never would have figured you for a marryin' man. Not when I first saw you out in the desert that day—taking down the deer I was tracking. At first, I thought you were Apache. Then I realized you were something even wilder. A half-breed. At home in no world. I couldn't have imagined you falling in love with any woman, much less my uppity sister." She smiled. "Maybe that's what made me so attracted."

"Well, I have." Yakima turned around, giving his back to the storm. He took a deep drag off his quirley and blew the smoke against the hovel's adobe front wall, which had a long, curved crack in it. "I'm in love with her. So, you and I, Emma, well…"

"He'll never allow it to happen, Yakima."

He narrowed a curious eye at her.

"Hugh Kosgrove will never allow it to happen." Emma had said these words slowly, enunciating each one carefully, a little snidely. "Poppa will never allow Julia to marry you."

Yakima just stared at her. Of course, he knew it was true.

Such was the nature of love—or what seemed to be a sprouting seed of love—that you never really thought it through. If he'd thought through his and Faith's love—a half-breed drifter and a beautiful former whore in the employ of the embittered Bill Thornton—they wouldn't have been together for as long as they had. It wouldn't have made any sense.

No, maybe Kosgrove wouldn't allow such a union. But there were places Yakima and Julia could go to get around such obstacles. Julia's and Kosgrove's relationship being as troubled as it now was, since she'd married Taggart—another man Kosgrove had deemed unworthy of his daughter's hand—Yakima doubted Julia would give two cents for what Kosgrove had to say on the matter.

He could make her and Yakima's life difficult in Apache Springs, but it was a big world. Kosgrove owned but a small chunk of it—the Conquistador.

"On the other hand," Emma said, reaching up to nudge his hat off his head so that it dropped down his back, where it hung by its braided horsehair thong, "he probably *would* let you marry me. Old Hugh Kosgrove's strict eastern rules don't apply to his younger, wilder daughter. He'd love for any man to tame me. Even a wild, green-eyed half-breed!"

"I don't know," Yakima said, tossing the stub of his cigarette out into the muddy yard. "He didn't want Taggart, a town marshal, to marry Julia. I doubt he'd want a wild, green-eyed savage to marry you." He looked at Emma. "I think you might think your old man has a lower opinion of you than he really does."

47

"How would you know?" she said defensively. "You've never even met the man."

Yakima gave her a wink. "Just got a sneaking suspicion, that's all."

Emma's cheeks colored a little, and she brushed her left breast against his arm. "Don't wink at me like that or I'll start pestering you again, you handsome devil." She turned her head a little to one side and narrowed one eye. "But if you try to plunder this canyon, I'll have to honor my promise to Jesus."

"Shoot me?"

She pressed her index finger against his chest. "Right through your brisket—solid as it is."

Yakima chuckled, then sagged into an old hemp-bottom chair, one leg of which was propped on a flat rock. "Don't worry. The wealth over yonder is way too much trouble for any man. Especially this man. Besides, when I get rich, I like to think it'll be more on account of hard work than plundering a church."

He sipped his coffee, then looked at Emma standing with her back against the gallery rail, arms crossed on her breasts, holding her coffee in one hand.

"I sort of thought you'd see it that way. I'm sorry I shot at you, Yakima. When I think I could have—"

"Tell me about this place, Emma. Tell me about Jesus. Just out of curiosity, you understand," he hastened to add with an ironic half smile, glancing at the New Line .41-caliber Colt revolver she wore strapped to her shapely hip.

She hiked her other hip onto the gallery rail, took another sip of her coffee, then stared out at the rain, which appeared to be lightening somewhat, the thunder dwindling, lightning forks growing less dramatic over the surrounding peaks. "I rode into this canyon the same way as you, looking for a way home. Jesus heard my horse, went for his rifle, fired a shot. Fortunately for me, his eyesight was going by then. He didn't know how old he was—his parents lost track of the years out here—but I figured that when I met him, five years ago, he was in his late sixties. Maybe even seventy."

Yakima had just finished building and firing another quirley. Emma stepped over to pluck the cigarette from between his fingers. She took a drag, half closing her pretty eyes, then blowing the smoke out into the slowly dying storm. She returned the cigarette to Yakima, then went inside for the coffee pot. When she'd refilled both of their cups and had set the pot on the rail beside her, she continued.

"Jesus's shot frightened my horse. He threw me. I wasn't as good on a horse then as I am now." She smirked at this, smiled, ran her index finger around on the rim of her refreshed cup. "Jesus was surprised to find a girl out here. I guess that's why he didn't kill me. He doctored my bruised hip and twisted ankle and helped me run down my horse. While he did, he swore me to secrecy and told me that he'd lived in the canyon all his life. His parents had, as well. He'd had a woman—several, in fact, but they were long dead. Jesus's family, as well as his wives, had been Apache slaves of the Jesuits who'd operated the mines that spotted that ridge up there. Back before the earthquake that collapsed the ridge and killed nearly all of the slaves but a few... including Jesus's grandfather and grandmother.

"The mines had been in operation for many years. Jesus wasn't sure how many. Much gold had been milled and smelted here and shipped back to Mexico City, and from there to Spain. Every ounce dug and milled by slave labor. After the earthquake that killed so many Apaches, one of the survivors, an Apache witch, led an insurgence of the surviving slaves against the Jesuits. When the priests had been killed and their bones scattered, she cursed this canyon. The gold that had been dug out of those mines by the dead slaves shall always remain here, in honor of their memory. No one will ever spend it for private gain. Any taken out of the canyon will cause death and destruction everywhere it goes.

"Most of the surviving slaves left the canyon after the quake, to freely live out their lives. The Apache witch and her husband and son stayed to protect the canyon from interlopers—from anyone who might find this hallowed ground and desecrate it by removing the gold. That son was Jesus's father, who married another former slave and remained here, true to his mother's wishes, after his parents had died."

Yakima stared in wide-eyed interest at Emma, as the words of the riveting, improbable tale dwindled from her lips.

"No kiddin'?" was all he could find to say after nearly a minute, the quirley drooping from a corner of his mouth.

The sky was only spitting now, the thunder rumbling into the distance.

Emma turned to him. "No kidding. Jesus married descendants of the slaves, their families still living in the area, trading with one another and with other Apaches both north and south of the border. All were sworn to secrecy about the existence of this canyon and the treasure here. Jesus married two more times. He had four children, but all died from one ailment or another. One I think died in a rockslide on the slope yonder, while trapping rattlesnakes, one of their primary foods. Then, after the years had passed... there was only Jesus... a broken-down, hump-backed old Mestizo—one-quarter Spanish-Mexican and three-quarters Mexican-Apache—when I met him. While he was dying from the snake poison, he asked me to take over for him here, in his people's plight."

"As protector of the canyon?"

Emma nodded.

Yakima sighed, chuckled softly, dubiously, and looked off, blowing smoke out toward the gallery's far end.

Emma frowned. "You don't believe me?"

"Oh, I don't doubt you were told that very tale," Yakima said. "I'm sure ole Jesus told you every word of what you just told me. It's Jesus I don't believe."

Emma looked indignant. "Why on earth not?"

"It's the oldest game in the gold-hunting book. Tell someone the canyon around your diggin's is haunted, they'll stay away. If they're the superstitious sort, that is. I'm not."

Still, he couldn't deny that feeling of evil he'd felt earlier.

"What? You think Jesus was just some old prospector who stumbled onto this place and concocted that story to keep others out?"

"It's happened before."

"Why wouldn't he have just taken as much treasure as he could carry and gotten out?"

"Maybe he was tryin' to figure a way to get it *all* out, without no one else gettin' suspicious."

"For three years?"

Yakima hiked a shoulder. He had to admit it sounded a little far-fetched. On the other hand, so did Jesus's story about the Apache witch's curse on the canyon, and the three generations of his family living out their lives here, watching over this place. He'd sat around many a campfire, listening to long windies blown by old prospectors, but Jesus's tale took the prize.

"Explain the church, then. All the treasure in there."

"Oh, I don't doubt there were mines around here. Probably up on the fallen-down ridge, even. A good chunk of that gold ended up in the church. For one reason or another, the Jesuits or Franciscans, or whoever built it, deserted it. Likely due to Apache or Yaqui raids. They probably planned to return for the gold one day, but it's a long way to Mexico City."

Emma was shaking her head and pursing her lips. "No. Jesus and I were friends. He would have told me the truth. Maybe not right away, but later he would have. I rode out here to visit that kind old man at least once every two weeks since I first stumbled on the canyon. I loved him. And he loved me, in his grandfatherly way. Besides, even if it was a lie, when he was dying, he would have told me the truth."

Emma shook her head again, stubbornly. "You're wrong, Yakima. There's a curse on this canyon. Deep down, you know it's true." She paused. When she spoke

53

again, her voice was pitched with low, quiet menace. "And you know what else?"

Yakima flicked his cigarette stub into the yard and leaned back in his chair, entwining his hands behind his head. "What?"

"I think someone knows about it and is trying to find it. One of them is who I thought you were. That's why I was so eager to trim your wick." Emma dropped to a knee before him and placed a hand on his thigh. "You have to help me keep them away, Yakima, or something really awful is going to happen!"

5

The next morning Yakima waited for the floodwaters of the previous night's storm to recede before saddling Wolf, loading up the two dead men, and following Emma west along the canyon floor. To his left, where previous floods had cut a second, slightly deeper floor in the canyon's center, the last of the floodwaters swirled and gurgled, sending up steam snakes to glisten like melting butter in the high desert sunshine.

After a half hour of slow riding along the base of the northern ridge, the ridge dropped away behind them, and the canyon narrowed and doglegged to the right.

For a moment, Yakima thought the canyon ended just ahead, in a giant rumble of black boulders sprouting tufts of greasewood, catclaw, and Mormon tea. But then Emma swung her buckskin to the far right, apparently finding an ancient trail of some sort, and Yakima followed, skirting the edge of the rubble, dropping into another shallow arroyo, then swinging sharply right—up a steep, gravelly bank.

The game trail twisted and turned until finally Yakima and Emma were out of the canyon.

They stopped on the canyon's lip, in a fringe of mesquites and palo verdes, to rest the horses. Yakima looked back down into the canyon. Only, from this vantage you really couldn't tell there was any canyon down there. It appeared like a narrow arroyo mounded over with boulders of all shapes and sizes.

"Perfectly hidden from this end," he said, half to himself. "No one could find a way into the canyon from here. And from the other end, about the only way you'd end up in the chasm is by accident."

"That's how I figure it." Emma shook her hair back, then turned to stare off to her left, behind and beyond Yakima. "Someone's been looking mighty hard, though."

"How do you know?"

Emma looked at him, then swung her right boot over her saddlehorn and dropped straight down to the ground. "Right this way."

Yakima dismounted, ground-reined Wolf, and followed the young woman around boulders and mesquites as well as saguaros and barrel cactus. He yawned as he walked, brushed a tired hand down his face.

His sleep had been troubled. He'd bedded down outside, on the shack's gallery, but knowing that Emma was inside, so close, had nettled the maleness in him no end. He was assaulted by discomfiting, remembered images of the times they'd spent together, before he'd begun tumbling for her sister. It didn't help hearing Emma moaning in her sleep only feet away from him, her own dreams likely assaulted by the same memories.

He brushed knuckles over the point of his chin, stifling a wry chuckle.

Ahead of him, Emma stopped suddenly and dropped to her haunches by a small pile of gray ashes from a recent campfire. Yakima looked around. There were a couple of discarded airtight tins and the charred bones of a small animal, probably a rabbit.

"So, someone camped out here," Yakima said. "Doesn't mean they were looking for the canyon."

"I wouldn't think so, either," Emma said, "if I hadn't seen two more campsites just like this one about a mile west, and two more on the other side of the canyon, near Hawk's Pass."

Yakima squatted beside Emma. He picked up a charred airtight tin and turned it between his gloved fingers, staring at it. He wondered if the Rio Grande Kid was the one who'd left this fire as well as the others. The Kid had ridden out this way several times with his dead pard

Eddie's treasure map in his pocket.

Yakima didn't think the Kid had been out here within the past couple of weeks, however. With all the folks pouring into Apache Springs of late, Yakima had needed all hands on deck. His only two hands at the moment were the Kid and Galveston Penny, a gun-savvy but good-natured and seemingly trustworthy young man, twenty-two years old, who'd taken the job Yakima had advertised in hand-written circulars he'd posted around town. Not long ago, it had become obvious that two town lawmen were no longer adequate to keep the growing population of Apache Springs buttoned down, so Yakima, with the permission of the city council, had added Penny as his second deputy.

All three lawmen—Yakima, the Rio Grande Kid, and the real kid, Penny—had had their hands full for the past several weeks. The Kid hadn't had time to head into the desert looking for his El Dorado. Yakima had scoffed at the idea of Eddie's treasure. He'd thought for sure Eddie had imagined the whole thing.

He didn't know what to think now. He wasn't sure what to make of that much treasure. Just the idea of so much wealth made his head feel light and his toes tingle. If the Kid ever saw that canyon, he'd likely get so excited he'd die of a heartstroke before he could get any of the gold out of it.

"What're you thinking about?"

Yakima dropped the can. "Nothin'." He didn't want Emma to know about the Kid's treasure map. She had her neck in such a kink about anyone stumbling into that canyon that she might ride into town and back shoot Yakima's older deputy. Of course, he thought he knew her well enough to doubt she'd really do that, but, given her seeming zealousness for keeping Jesus's secret, part of him wondered.

She was a wild one, Emma.

"What is it?" she coaxed, staring at him curiously. "Tell me."

Yakima straightened with a sigh. "I was just thinking it might be wise for you to let this whole thing go. The canyon, I mean. You don't live out here. Your home is the Conquistador. You don't owe Jesus or that canyon a damn thing. If someone finds it, let 'em find it."

Emma straightened, her eyes nearly crossing as she regarded Yakima with her customary defiance. She slid a lock of flaxen hair back away from the mole on her cheek that gave her face bewitching definition. "I can't do that. I know you don't understand, but I can't, and that's that. As long as I live anywhere near this canyon, and as long as I'm still alive, I am going to do everything I can to make sure that treasure stays where it is."

She brushed past Yakima and stomped back to where

the horses grazed mesquite beans near the canyon's lip.

"It's a mighty big responsibility," Yakima called after her in frustration. "I don't think Jesus knew what he was askin' you to do, is all I'm sayin'." Never mind that he didn't believe in the curse anyway.

Emma just kept walking, not so much as glancing over her shoulder at him.

Yakima followed her back to the horses. She was already mounted.

"Head back that way," she said, jerking her chin toward a crease between two small, shelving mesas straight north of the canyon. "You'll pick up the trail to Apache Springs in a half hour." She flared a nostril. "Don't get lost again."

She swung her buckskin around and nudged it west through the rocks and gravelly mounds of red grit spiked with cacti, presumably heading back to the Conquistador. Yakima grabbed the reins of the dead men's horses and mounted Wolf. He turned to see that Emma had stopped the buckskin and turned around to face him.

A saucy smirk tugged at her mouth corners.

"How did you sleep last night?" she asked, jeering.

"Terrible."

"Good!" She spat the word out, half laughing, half cajoling, then neck-reined the buckskin around once more and spurred it into a gallop.

Soon she was gone. Then there was just Yakima, Wolf,

the dead men and their horses, a loud cicada, and the hot sun beating down. Beyond, to the south, lay the hidden canyon in which wealth too vast for him to imagine was shrouded by the ancient church. As he stared in that direction, a raw fear gnawed at him.

When he'd first spied the treasure, he'd known the ache of gold fever. The fever was tempered by his knowing that he had no use for so much gold. He hadn't realized it, but aside from Faith having been taken from him, he was pretty much satisfied with his life as it was.

His gold fever had been replaced by a churning apprehension. What would happen to whoever found that wealth and hauled it out of the canyon? Of course, someday it would be found. When it was, it would forever change whoever found it, and it would forever change everyone around that person or those people. The entire town of Apache Springs, most likely. As far as Yakima was concerned, the town was changing, growing fast enough, as it was.

He had the undeniable feeling that the treasure down there was like a massive keg of black powder just waiting for its fuse to be lit. And when it exploded, it would take out half of the county. Yakima didn't believe in the curse.

On the other hand, maybe he did.

The feeling of something evil down there had been real. Maybe it was the lingering, tortured souls of the slaves who'd been forced to mine the canyon until they'd died meaninglessly in the quake. Whatever caused the feeling, Yakima didn't care ever to visit that canyon again.

He switched his gaze toward where Emma had shown him the remains of the campfire. She was probably right. Someone was looking for the treasure. Whoever it was, they were getting close. If they kept looking, they'd find it.

How did they know it was down there? Did they have a map?

The questions lingered in the half-breed's mind as he urged Wolf forward and, leading the two dead men's horses by their bridle reins, began riding to Apache Springs.

Soon, he picked up the main horse trail and followed it through the chaparral, climbing up and over hills and steep, rocky hogbacks. The air was warm and humid from last night's storm. The arroyos were still muddy. Steam rose from them. All around, the intermingling peaks of the Chiricahuas and Sierra Estrada jutted, dark-green and light-yellow with distance, shadows sliding across them.

A hunting Mexican buzzard, a *zopilate,* gave its ratcheting cry.

Ahead, the half-breed could see the high rocky pass on which sprawled the burgeoning town of Apache Springs. The pass was the southern entrance to the Sierra Estrada. To the southwest of the pass, bristling desert rolled away to the Southern Pacific rails forty miles distant. Those rails connected Tucson to Lordsburg in the east, and vice versa. In fact, they connected both coasts, an idea that, for Yakima, born when the Iron Horse was still a foggy notion even in the minds of its creators, was nearly as hard to fathom as the wealth in the canyon he'd put behind him.

Slowly, the trail rose until he found himself on the Apache Springs pass, with the town now dead ahead, sprawling up and down the several rises rolling up and away to the last rise of the pass a mile or so beyond. He reined up on a high hill, on the southeast corner of the town. Wolf curveted, and Yakima rested his right hand on his right thigh, near where his .44's holster was tied to his muscular leg swelling out his denim pant leg, and stared out over the town.

His town.

Yes, it had come to feel like that now. No one could have been more surprised than himself. He'd never felt at home anywhere before. At least, not in any town and not around more than a handful of people. But, for some reason, he felt at home here. Which wasn't to say that the decidedly reddish hue of his skin and the raptor-like cast of his nose didn't cause him to be looked down on by more than a few from time to time right here in Apache Springs.

Still, he and the town, in its earlier, pre-burn guise, as well as in this current rebuilt, booming manifestation, had been through a lot together. Yakima had known many of the people who'd died here in the fire, just as he knew many of the fire's survivors. (There were far too few of those.) He'd come to know many more people who'd poured in over the past months, after gold had been discovered north and west of the pass.

Those newcomers had seen him more as a native of Apache Springs than a lowly aborigine. He supposed he really was a native of the town in a way, having helped rebuild the place. For that reason, folks tended to be more accepting than if he'd been a stranger riding into town for the first time.

Of course, it also helped that he wore a badge and carried its authority on his shoulders. On the other hand, there were a few here and there who resented a redskin bearing any authority at all, much less the authority of a badge-toting town marshal. Because of that attitude, he'd had to bust a few heads. He'd likely have to bust a few more in the weeks and months, maybe years, ahead.

Just the same, he'd sunk a taproot here in Apache Springs, if only a little ways down beneath the thin volcanic soil. It felt good. He didn't doubt that he'd tire of the place, or that it would tire of him, and he'd eventually ride on. At the moment he felt the warm, familiar feeling of having a home, of belonging in and to a place, and of having a definite connection with others.

That thought got him thinking of Julia Taggart and, as he booted Wolf on down the hill and into the outskirts of the town, the pounding of hammers rising all around him as more houses and businesses were going up, he glanced over his left shoulder. The cemetery in which Julia's dead husband lay buried rose in the north, stippled with rocks, mesquites, and palo verdes. A path climbed the cemetery hill, the base of which was delineated by a freshly painted white picket fence.

Yakima remembered finding her there, just after Lon had been shot in front of both her and Yakima, in the town jailhouse, and how her grief had been so deep and poignant that it had made her want to stay there in the cemetery, despite the monsoon rain lashing her, soaking her to the bone. Yakima had taken her back to her house and, for good or bad, right or wrong, they'd made love that day, weathering the storm of each other's shared grief.

They'd made love many times after that, and it was with a tug of lust in his loins now that he glanced toward her house as he rode on into what was now the heart of Apache Springs, at the broad, flat area atop the rocky pass. He couldn't see her house from this vantage, at the corner of Main Street and Third Avenue, because more houses had gone up recently, blocking his view. But the lovely Julia's neat frame house stood along the former unnamed trail that now bore the official moniker of Third Avenue.

Julia was likely home now, in the early afternoon, going about her chores. Yakima would pay her a visit soon, after he'd dealt with Goose McGowan and Curly Buck, and tended his and the dead men's horses. He'd stop by to tell her he was back in town, because she'd likely been worried about him.

Maybe he'd have a piece of pie and a cup of coffee, and they'd sit together out in the hanging wooden swing Lon had built for himself and Julia, beneath a brush *ramada* in their backyard. Just a short visit. Yakima had work to do. He would stop back later in the evening, and he and the pretty widow, and older sister of the wild Emma, would make tender love in her canopied bed.

Now he let Wolf pick his own way through the early afternoon traffic. There seemed to be more and more ranch wagons in town every week, for the land on the south side of the pass, with its springs and its wealth of grama grass and good hay pastures along the Rio Estrada, was coveted ranch country. Much of the traffic Yakima wove through now, however, was that of drays loaded with fresh, green-smelling lumber freighted up from the Southern Pacific rails and being off-loaded at the various building sites around Apache Springs.

There were also many prospectors' wagons and, in

some cases, prospectors' handcarts being pushed by burly, bushy-bearded desert rats, some with a mongrel dogging the heels of their worn, high-topped leather boots.

There were all the sounds of a rollicking boomtown— men shouting boisterously; half-dressed painted ladies laughing on second- and third-floor balconies and on boardwalks fronting the town's numerous saloons, including the sprawling, rebuilt Busted Flush Saloon & Dance Hall. Piano music, some of it not bad, pushed through batwing doors. Dogs barked. Horses whinnied, and mules brayed. Hooves beat a steady rhythm all through the day and often into the night.

There was the hammering of nails from all directions, and the cacophony of blacksmiths' hammers, for all the wagons rolling through town often needed new axles or wheel rims, and the horses and mules needed shoeing. At last count, Yakima deemed there were at least three blacksmiths now serving Apache Springs, which had been little more than freshly charred ruins less than two years ago.

There was another sound. Others like it were growing more and more common despite Yakima's attempts at keeping the violence tamped down.

It was the sound of gunfire.

More specifically, it was the thunderous concussion of a shotgun.

Just then a man was blasted out of the large louvered doors of the Busted Flush on Yakima's right, propelled across the saloon's broad wooden veranda without his feet even touching the floor, to hit the street not ten feet in front of Wolf, where the shotgun-blasted man rolled, screaming, in a cloud of dust.

6

Yakima looked from the man in the street to the Busted Flush, a big, beautiful building in its new transformation, sitting across the side street from Señora Galvez's Place—a purple, mansard-roofed affair with red gingerbread trim, a broad front gallery painted glistening white, and a white balcony running around its second story. A red lamp shone in a window near the front door.

Boots thumped inside the Flush, the sounds growing louder.

Yakima began to reach for the Yellowboy, but then the Rio Grande Kid stopped just inside the louvered doors and stared out over the batwings, his big, beefy face, as craggy as a coffee tin used for target practice, flushed in anger. He looked at the man he'd apparently shot.

The man was no longer screaming. In fact, he was no longer doing much of anything except lying belly up in the street. Yakima and a couple of wagons had stopped near him, while the rest of the traffic continued as usual.

Yakima looked at the Kid, who was pushing sixty or sixty-five. His age was a carefully kept secret, just as he shrouded his own identity in a myth of his own making. The half-breed lawman said, "I see you've been keeping busy. I was worried you might go fishing as soon as I left town."

The Kid shook his head as he stepped through the batwings and tugged his funnel-brimmed, badly weathered Stetson down low on his warty, liver-spotted forehead. "I was thinkin' about it, but then all hell broke loose up at the new Chinese brothel down by the wash. And then it was payday out to the Bridlebit, and all the boys rode to town to stomp with their tails up. As if that wasn't bad enough, that *hombre* there's been spoilin' for a fight in every saloon he's walked into. Snake-oil salesman, though I think he done drunk up all his inventory. Most places kicked him out, including Cleve Dundee over here at the Flush."

Dundee himself pushed out the batwings to stand on his broad front gallery beside the Kid. Like his saloon, Dundee had received a makeover. He stood a few inches taller than the Kid beside him, a big man, bald as an egg, now sporting a nattily tailored suit of clothes complete with pinstriped shirt with a poet's collar and arm bands, and creased broadcloth trousers. The black, gold-buckle shoes on his feet glistened in the desert sunshine from a recent polishing and buffing.

He once wore a tangled beard. The beard was gone—or at least transformed. Now, thick muttonchops dragged down the sides of his broad, pale, raw-boned face to angle over and connect in a thick, waxed, handlebar mustache mantling his mouth. Even the patch, worn over the socket of the eye he'd lost in Rebel Wilkes's sacking of the town, gave him a rough-and-tumble, big-city businessman's air of intrigue.

"But then he came back," the saloon owner said, adjusting the black patch over his left eye as he gazed into the street at the presumably dead man. "I guess he thought he'd start all over again. He pulled a gun on me, so I sent for the Kid."

"He pulled a gun on me," the Kid said, spattering a wad of chaw over the gallery's front rail, "so I aired him out a little." He held up his big, double-barreled Greener in both hands across his thick, lumpy chest and grinned.

The quick thuds of running boots sounded, and Yakima began to automatically reach for the Yellowboy again, but stopped the motion when he saw Galveston Penny running toward the Busted Flush from the west, on the same side of the street the Flush was on. He was a slender, fresh-faced lad in dark-brown trousers, dress shirt, string tie, and bowler hat. The well-liked young Penny, or Master Galveston, as he was called by everyone in town, had had his fill of "wet-nursing beeves on the hoof," as he called cow-punching and which he'd been doing since not long after graduating from rubber pants on a west Texas tumbleweed farm.

That's why he'd applied for the job as second town marshal and burned his impossibly dusty, smelly, and faded range clothes an hour after he'd donned the badge. He'd burned everything but his worn brown boots, that is. He'd said the boots fit him like moccasins, and it was so rare to break in a pair of boots "so good your feet called 'em by their first names" that he couldn't part with the rundown, undershot Dan Posts, though they did stand in sharp contrast to the rest of his sharper, more city-bred attire.

Twenty-two years old, young Penny didn't look a day older than twenty. He was a slender, tow-headed, blue-eyed young man roughly six feet tall, two inches taller than the oldster, the Rio Grande Kid. The two pearl-gripped Colts he'd bought at a local gun store as soon as he'd landed the job, and for which Yakima was sure he was still in hock, sagged in thonged-down, hand-tooled leather holsters on both bowed thighs. In his hands just now was the brush-scarred Winchester carbine he'd carried on the range.

His blue eyes flashed anxiously as he stopped near the bottom of the Busted Flush's front steps, glanced from the Kid to Yakima and then to do the dead man in the street.

"Heard the shootin'," he said, breathless from his run. "What happened?"

"That varmint tried to take me to the dance," the Kid told him.

"That snake-oil salesman?" young Penny said.

The Kid nodded as he broke open his shotgun and plucked out the spent shells. "He milked oil from his last snake."

Galveston laughed. He'd taken to the Kid like a toddler to rock candy. He thought everything the Kid said was at once humorous and wise, believed all the Kid's tales of his rowdy outlaw days, and the Kid basked in the younger man's admiration.

"Where you been?" Yakima asked Penny.

The youngest deputy jerked his chin to indicate the northwest side of town. "A coupla riders from the Bridlebit went hog wild this morning on their way out of town and busted up Mister Patten's picket fence. Mister Patten wanted me to check it out, and he wants the culprits run to justice. I was out askin' around if there were any witnesses, but it was awful dark last night. No one got a good look at the miscreants."

Ralph Patten owned the First Bank of Apache

Springs. He and his wife had moved here from the Midwest to open a new bank, replacing the one that had been looted and burned by Wilkes's bunch. Patten's wife suffered from consumption, and her doctor had prescribed the move to a dryer, warmer climate. They'd built a stately brick, Victorian-style house two blocks north and west of Main Street.

Yakima had pulled Wolf and the other two horses over to where the Kid stood in front of the Busted Flush and turned to Penny, standing on the broad main street's other side.

"Inquire with the bartenders around town," he told the young deputy as he swung down from the saddle, raising his voice to be heard above the clatter of traffic. "Find out which Bridlebit riders left town around the same time that fence was ruined. When you see those riders again, tell them they can either buy the materials and replace Patten's fence or spend a week in the hoosegow."

He jerked the Yellowboy from his saddle scabbard and rested the rifle on his shoulder.

Young Penny pinched his hat brim and started to turn away, but Yakima stopped him. "First, get that snake-oil salesman off the street. And take Curly Buck and Goose over to the undertaker's. Have 'em fitted for wooden overcoats. Tell Jenkins the town'll likely be paying for their planting, so his cheapest model will suffice. When you're done with that, you can stable Wolf and these other two horses."

He turned to the Kid, who'd come down the gallery steps to stand beside him on the boardwalk. "Me an' the Kid need to powwow back at the office."

When Galveston Penny had led the three horses off in the direction of the new undertaking parlor, Yakima and the Rio Grande Kid began slanting across the street to the east, heading for the barrack-like adobe-brick town marshal's office, identified by a sign stretching into the street on two cottonwood poles. The sign was the only thing new about the place. The fire had avoided the jail-house, so it was the same rudimentary building that Lon Taggart had operated from.

There was a new city hall, but the parsimonious town boosters had seen no reason to make a jailhouse part of it when the standing one worked just fine for holding prisoners, never mind that it was often too small to hold all the criminals Yakima and his deputies found themselves arresting on a wild, drunken Saturday night.

"What're we powwowin' about, Marshal?" the Kid asked as he followed Yakima up the four steps to the adobe hovel's small, brush-roofed front gallery. "Don't tell me the town boosters caught wind of my criminal past and ordered you to fire me. Or, worse, arrest me!"

"No, no—nothin' like that." Yakima tripped the latch

and opened the door.

"Whew!" The Kid shook his head as though with relief as he followed Yakima into the office flanked by four barred jail cages. "I thought I was gonna have to shoot my way out of another town. That gets old when you're gettin' on in years!" He turned to the window by the door and used his double-barreled Greener to slide the flour-sack curtain to one side as he stared out. "And, I don't know what it is, but I've grown to fancy this town."

Yakima hooked his hat on a wall peg by the door. "Maybe, at your age, you've just grown to fancy a steady, honest job and a roof over your head. Even if that roof does belong to a whore's crib most of the time."

The Kid wheezed a laugh, moving his heavy, rounded shoulders as he turned to face the half-breed lawman. "That might have somethin' to do with it—sure enough. And a steady paycheck is novel for this old border bandit." He chuckled again, then leaned his shotgun against the wall and hooked his thumbs behind his cartridge belt. "What're we powwowin' about, Yak?"

Neither man took much stock in formalities. They were partners first, town marshal and deputy second.

Yakima wasn't sure how to ask the question without arousing the Kid's suspicion. Maybe there was no way to do it, so he just came out with it. "Where's your map?"

The Kid's bushy, gray-stitched, red-brown brows slid

down over his eyes. "Huh?"

"Your treasure map. You know—the one you keep in your Bible? The one your friend Eddie drew."

"The one I—?" The Kid looked astounded. "How in tarnation did you know I kept it in my Bible?"

"You were a better bank robber than you are a secret keeper, Kid." Yakima moved to the roll-top desk that served both deputies and that sat against a wall by the line of jail cells, near a sandbox for chaw. The town marshal crouched, drew open a bottom drawer, and lifted out a one-foot-high stack of *Policeman's Gazette* illustrated magazines, the Kid's favorite reading material, though Yakima suspected he mainly looked at the pictures.

The Kid stared at the open drawer in shock. "How did you know—?"

"That you 'hide' the map in your Bible, under these magazines?" Yakima snorted wryly. "Just check it."

"Huh?"

"Check the Bible."

The Kid crouched over the drawer, reached inside with his two ham-sized, dirt-colored, freckled and liver-spotted hands, and from within it drew an old, falling-apart Bible sprouting yellowed papers with spidery, inked writing, most in a woman's flowery hand. "This is the Bible my dear mother gave me on her deathbed, nigh on twenty years ago. One of the few times I wasn't doin' time in a state or territorial pen somewhere. It's the Day Family Bible."

"Check it."

"Huh?"

Yakima sighed in frustration. "Look in the back and see if your precious map is still there."

"How did you know—?"

"Just check the damned thing!"

The Kid opened the book, looked inside the back cover, then flipped through the pages near the back, and his lower jaw sagged farther and farther toward his chest. He looked in wide-eyed shock at Yakima. "It ain't there!" He glanced around at the floor as though the old scrap of paper might have fallen out.

"Shit," Yakima said.

"How did you... how did you know it was gone?"

"Had me a feelin'." Yakima moved to the window and stared out in frustration.

"Come on, Yak," the Kid urged. "How did you know the map was there in the first place, and then how did you know it was *gone?*"

Yakima turned toward the beefy old deputy. "Hell, you sit there and ogle that map all the time. We can have a jail full of prisoners, and you still pull that old Bible out, bite off a chunk of wedding cake, and sit there and chew and spit and stare at that map like it's a picture of a half-clad fallen angel. When you're through, you always get that guilty look on your big, ugly mug, look around, then stick the map in the back of the Bible and stuff the Bible under your magazines. I've seen you pull that stunt a dozen times."

"Shit!"

"I hope you were a better bank robber, though all the time you did behind bars doesn't say much in your favor."

"I was a hellion at robbin' banks!" the Kid intoned, defensively. "I ain't been old an' stupid all my life! Now, tell me how you knew it was gone." He stepped up close to Yakima, like a bull ready to burst through a chute. He turned his head to one side and narrowed one suspicious eye. "Did you steal it? If so, all bets are off!" He brushed his right hand across the top of his old, holstered Remington, freeing the keeper thong from over the hammer.

"Yeah, I stole it," Yakima said with another wry chuckle. "That's why I just showed you it was gone. Because I'm no smarter than you are."

The Kid turned his head to the other side and narrowed his other eye, which flickered uncertainly. "You're startin' to confuse me now."

"That don't take much." Yakima walked behind Taggart's old desk facing out from the far adobe wall on which a framed map of Arizona Territory hung, flanked by flags of both Arizona Territory and a thirty-eightstarred red-white-and-blue.

He plopped down in the swivel chair behind the desk, peeled off his gloves, hiked his boots onto the edge of the desk, and crossed them at the ankles. The desk was littered with all kinds of paperwork, most of which he wouldn't have had any inclination of doing even if he'd known how to do it. To hell with it. His job was to keep the tough nuts from running wild and trampling the banker's picket fence.

And, since yesterday, to keep the Wildcat of the Sierra Estrada from getting herself or anyone else killed.

He glanced at the line of empty cells on his left, then turned to the Kid, who stood staring in open-mouthed exasperation at the old Bible in his hands.

"Who'd you have in here over the last two days?"

The Kid lifted his head slowly to stare back at Yakima. "Huh?"

"Think about it. Who'd you have in here over the last couple of days? The day I left…" He let his voice trail off, then crossed his arms on his chest and shook his head. "Ah, hell. Whoever took your map took it a lot longer ago than that."

If the same person or persons who'd taken the map had also left the remains of the campfires Emma had spotted near the canyon, they'd have to have taken the map quite a while ago. At least a week ago. Probably even more than that.

"You think whoever took it was in one of our cells?" the Kid asked, his voice thin with bewilderment. He sounded like a little boy whose best friend had just left town for good.

"No doubt. Who else… besides myself, that is… would know you keep it in your Bible… and that you keep your Bible in the bottom drawer of that desk?"

"Ah, hell!" The Kid walked over to the window by the door, rested his elbows on the sill, and pressed his fists against his temples. "I'm such a damn fool!" He stared out for a time, then turned to Yakima again, his craggy face creased with suspicion and curiosity. "Say, now… how did you know it was gone?"

Yeah, how did Yakima know the map wouldn't be in the Kid's Bible?

"Just had a feelin'," he muttered, running a fingernail along the edge of the desk and turning askance from the Kid's skeptical gaze.

"Just had a feelin', huh?" The Kid wasn't buying it. He walked slowly toward the desk, his face a mask of wariness and suspicion. "What was it that gave you the—?"

Yakima couldn't have been more pleased when boots thudded on the front gallery and spurs rang, causing the Kid to break off his interrogation. Galveston Penny opened the front door and walked inside, poking his crisp new bowler hat, which appeared one size too small, back from his pale forehead. "Them two dead owl hoots and the horses done been taken care of, Marshal Henry. I ran into Señora Galvez on the way over here. She seen you was back in town, and she wondered if we told you about…" Young Galveston let the thought dwindle on his lips as he turned to the Kid. "You told him, didn't you, Kid?"

"Told him?" the Kid said, still preoccupied with his concern over the missing map. "Told him about what?"

"What Señora Galvez said. You know—about a possible holdup or somesuch. Somethin' big bein' planned for Apache Springs!"

Yakima dropped his feet to the floor and rested his elbows on the arms of the swivel chair. "What're you talkin' about, Galveston?"

"Oh, yeah!" The Kid snapped his fingers in the air, remembering. "I done forgot about Señora Galvez."

"What about her?" Yakima prodded the pair.

"She come in here yesterday all distraught," young Penny said. "She said one of her girls overheard a couple of fellas—a couple of customers—over to Señora Galvez's place talkin' about doin' a big job around here somewheres. Sounded like they was talkin' about a hold-up, and it sounded like it was gonna happen soon. She wanted to warn you."

"Yeah, yeah," the Kid said. "She said she'd like it if you'd go over and powwow with her personal."

"She seemed a mite concerned," Penny added.

"All right." Yakima rose from his chair, glad to have

83

an excuse to clear out of the office for a while. At least until he could come up with a convincing lie to tell the Kid about how he'd known the map was missing from his Bible. He grabbed his gloves, stuffed them into a back pocket, then pulled his hat off the peg by the door and set it on his head. "You two mind the store."

"Uh…" said Galveston Penny, shambling toward Yakima. The young man smiled bashfully and said, "You… uh… wouldn't let me tag along with you, would you, Marshal Henry?"

"Tag along?"

"Yeah, you know…"

"Not exactly, no."

The Kid laughed.

Penny's smooth, open face flushed deep crimson.

Then Yakima understood. He'd seen young Galveston chinning with one of the girls in front of Señora Galvez's place—a pretty little Mexican girl named Clara, if Yakima remembered right. The younker had been lit up like a Christmas tree. He'd lit up even brighter when young Clara, clad in a black-and-red corset and bustier and long, fishnet stockings, had taken his bowler and set it on her own head and flounced around, modeling it for him.

"Galveston," Yakima said, genuinely puzzled, "why don't you just save up your pennies and buy yourself a poke?"

The young man frowned, flushed, shook his head, and waved his hands, palm out. "No, no… I couldn't do that."

"Why not?"

"I just couldn't, that's all."

"Well, hell, boy," the Kid said, "the rest of the town does." He laughed again.

"It ain't like that… between her an' me," Galveston said.

"Like what?"

"Like that," Yakima said, suddenly understanding, remembering how, long ago, he'd once tumbled for a pretty *dove du pave* himself. Only, his had been a tall, slender, buxom blonde with cornflower-blue eyes—eyes as blue as blue wildflowers in a sunlit spring meadow—named Faith. Despite her profession, he'd tumbled for her hard, every bit as hard, or harder, than young Galveston Penny had apparently tumbled for Clara.

He knew how love, the kind of love that bit you deep down at your core, penetrated way beyond thoughts of a mere mattress dance.

"I still don't understand," the Kid said, shaking his head and running a hand down his face in frustration. "The world's a-changin' a mite fast for this old Kid, I reckon. When a young, strappin' young man ain't savin' his pennies to bleed off his sap with a comely Mescin whore"—he shook his head again in defeat—"what in tarnation is the world comin' to?"

"Galveston," Yakima said. "You don't need to hound-dog me over there. You go over there yourself tomorrow morning, before you go on duty, and bring her a spray of flowers and ask her out for breakfast. The girl's likely sleeping right now, and she'll be busy later tonight. Go on over there in the morning, wake her gently, and take her out for breakfast. She'd appreciate that better than anything else you could do for her."

"You think so?" Galveston said, staring at Yakima now with interest, but also with skepticism.

The half-breed lawman curled a conspiratorial half grin and winked. "Take it from me. I know. Now, why don't you go on over to Patten's place and assure him we're workin' on his picket fence." He winked again, then stepped outside.

As he drew the door closed behind him, the Kid called from the other side of it, "I still wanna know how you knew my map was missin', *Marshal Henry*!"

Yakima winced as he drew his cartridge belt up higher on his hips and tramped down the gallery steps. He slant-ed across the street toward Señora Galvez's place sitting across the side street from the Busted Flush.

He went inside and found the place understandably quiet—as quiet as a crypt, in fact, with the drapes drawn over the parlor windows, no lamps lit, and not a soul except a long-haired, smoke-colored cat and the Chinese cook moving around on the first floor. The air was spiced with Spanish incense, also known as marijuana, as well as a cloying potpourri of cigar smoke, man sweat, and cheap bottled fragrances. Yakima gave the cat, lounging on the back of a red velvet sofa by a cold fireplace, a friendly pat, then went into the kitchen and learned from the cook that Señora Galvez was in her boudoir upstairs, enjoying *siesta* along with the rest of the girls.

Yakima should have remembered. The Spanish madam's *siestas,* which all her girls enjoyed, as well, were well known around Apache Springs. They lasted from between one and five in the afternoon.

Such nap times made sense, given a whore's hours. The cook, a stocky man named Gu Cheng, but whom everyone called "Chang," said he'd wake her if Yakima thought it necessary, but Yakima could tell from the man's expression that rousting the madam from *siesta* was not to be done without just cause and might very well be met with no little Old Country rancor.

Yakima shook his head.

"I'll be back in a few hours," he told Chang, who, clad in a long smock over threadbare balbriggans, a loosely rolled quirley dangling from his mouth, was chopping rabbit meat and tossing the chunks into a stew pot bubbling on his coal-black range.

Yakima took his leave and headed back outside.

He studied the street for a time, wondering if what the madam had heard was true. He'd had to parry no hold-up attempts since his second time taking over the town marshal's job.

Then, again, the town was new. Newly reborn, anyway. Trouble was about to come from one quarter or another. The local lawdog would like to know which quarter he should be keeping an eye on.

Oh, well. He'd learn soon enough. He didn't want to wake Señora Galvez and risk rubbing her the wrong way. As owner of possibly the most lucrative business in Apache Springs so far, aside from the Busted Flush and the new mercantile, half-owned by Emma's and Julia's father, Hugh Kosgrove, the *señora* carried considerable weight. She tended to run hot and cold and could hold a grudge, fairly typical of South-of-the-Border ladies. At least, he'd heard she could cloud up and rain all over anyone who crossed her, or whom she perceived to have crossed her.

Yakima hadn't tangled with her so far, and he didn't care to. She was one of those women, not unlike the Wildcat of the Sierra Estrada, he'd rather wrestle a wounded grizzly bear than get crossways with.

He started retracing his steps to the marshal's office, then, thinking about the Kid possibly waiting there for him to continue grilling him about the map, Yakima switched course. He headed east, tramping across Second Avenue to the next cross street. Nearly to the edge of the business district, he headed north.

He swerved into a dry wash and followed its snaking course back west for fifty yards. He felt foolish for taking this roundabout way to his lover's house—this furtive route—but he sensed it best if not too many of Apache Springs's citizens knew that the half-breed marshal was paying visits to Julia Taggart, the former marshal's widow and Hugh Kosgrove's older daughter.

Yakima might have been town marshal, but his skin hadn't grown any lighter since he'd pinned the badge to his shirt. In fact, he was probably crazy for continuing to see Julia. Where could it lead, anyway? Still, he felt compelled. Julia had been on his mind ever since he'd left town. He suspected he was on hers. He wanted to let her know he was back.

He didn't like it being that way, he and Julia hailing from opposite sides of the tracks, as it were, and knowing that their relationship would eventually have to end— probably sooner rather than later.

But there it was.

He stepped out from between two palo verdes and glanced around to make sure neither of Julia's two near neighbors were in their backyards. Then he strode past Julia's privy and the brush *ramada* Lon had built, with the two-person swing hanging beneath it, and mounted the small stoop at Julia's back door.

He glanced around once more, then knocked twice on the door lightly. He turned the knob. The door opened. He stepped inside, into the cheerfully sunlit kitchen at the rear of the house.

"Julia?"

There was a shrill gasp, and then he saw her. She'd just stepped into the kitchen from the parlor, wrapped in a heavy towel, her brown hair pinned in a rich, messy pile atop her head, stray strands curling down against her pale, beautifully sculpted cheeks. Now she leaped back against the wall, jostling several pots and pans hanging from pegs, and splayed a hand across the two mounds of her breasts pushing out against the towel wrapped tightly against her torso, leaving bare her legs from below her thighs.

"I'm sorry," Yakima said quickly, doffing his hat and holding it against his chest. He extended his other hand apologetically. "I didn't mean to frighten you."

"Well, frighten me you certainly did, Yakima Henry! You're lucky I don't have a gun in here. If I did, I'd likely have shot you!" Recovering, she pushed off the wall and walked lithely over to him on her bare feet. She shoved his hat back and leaned close, pressing her cheek against his chest. "I'm so glad to see you. I had a dream about you last night. I dreamed that you were in trouble… out there in the desert."

"No trouble. At least none this unlikely lawdog couldn't take care of."

She looked up at him. "You found those two men who cut the girl at Señora Galvez's place?"

"Sure did." Yakima tucked a stray lock of her hair behind her ear. "They won't be cutting any more whores."

"That's good to hear. Those poor girls have it tough enough as it is without getting cut by drunk border toughs." Julia stepped back and looked up at him curiously. "Why did you come to the back door, Yakima? You do know this house comes with a front door, don't you?"

Yakima shrugged. "Just figured… you know…"

"No, I don't know."

Changing the subject, Yakima ran his hands down her long, slender arms and looked at the towel barely covering half of her. "I like the new duds."

Julia lifted a mouth corner, wryly. "I was hoping you'd be back today. I wanted to be freshly bathed for the occasion. Also…" She glanced at a steaming round pan resting on a warming rack of the range. "I made sweet rolls spiced liberally with cinnamon." She lifted her arms and placed her hands against the back of his neck, rising up on the tips of her small, pink toes, and kissed him. "Because I know you like cinnamon."

91

"Sweet rolls? What about pie?"

Julia stared at him for a moment, then shook her head slightly. "No more pie. At least, not for a while. You and I will be having sweet rolls with our afternoon coffee."

Yakima understood. The afternoon pie and coffee had been a holdover from her time with Lon. Making the buns instead of the pie was her way of saying she was letting go of the past and embracing the future.

Yakima dipped his head to kiss her wrist, which was fresh and clean from her bath and tasted vaguely of lemon. "Sweet rolls it is." He sniffed the air. "They sure do smell good."

"I took a little nap in the tub, and, when I woke up, I couldn't remember if I'd taken them out of the range or not. I came back down to check. I was just about to go back up and dress."

"I'll wait outside. I smell like sweat and horses, and I got enough trail dust on me to fill an Arizona canyon."

"You go on upstairs, and I'll heat water for a bath."

"You don't need to do that."

"I want to."

"Your water still up there?"

"Yes, but I'll throw it out."

"No need."

"What?"

"No need." Yakima snorted a laugh and drew her firmly

against him, running his hands down her slender, curving back to her rump lightly encased by the towel. "I'd find it an honor to bathe in your used bathwater, Miss Taggart."

Julia laughed, her gray eyes flashing. "Don't be silly!"

Yakima kissed her forehead, stepped around her, and strode across the kitchen and into the parlor. "I'll see ya upstairs!"

"You idiot! I'll bring the buns and coffee!"

"Can't wait!"

Upstairs in Julia's house, in her small but comfortably appointed bedroom—the bedroom she once shared with Lon, a fact Yakima did his best to try to forget, especially when they were making love in her and Lon's canopied bed—he unbuckled his cartridge belt and hung it over a chair back. He shucked out of his clothes and left them in a dirty pile on the floor by the bed. He'd take them over to a Chinese washhouse later, but, in the meantime, he needed to get his big, red, battle-scarred carcass scrubbed clean.

He was standing in the tub, lathering his legs with a chunk of scented soap and a soft cotton washcloth, when footsteps sounded in the hall outside the door, which he'd left open a foot. Julia nudged the door open with a bare toe and came in carrying a tray bearing two buns and two steaming coffee cups and saucers and a shallow bowl of creamy butter.

"Here we are," she said, setting the tray on a table near the bed.

She turned to him, sidestepped over to the bed, and sat down on the edge of it, tucking one long leg beneath the other one.

Yakima glanced at her twice, then his gaze held on hers. "What is it?"

"Nothing." She gave a coy little smile and nibbled her thumbnail. "I enjoy seeing you naked, that's all."

Yakima dropped the soap and the cloth in the water and straightened. "You have me at a disadvantage."

Her smile broadened. She cast her admiring gaze across his broad, wet shoulders, then down his hard, lumpy chest and across his flat belly to his soap-lathered, half-erect manhood and balls, hanging heavy now with raw male lust. She slid her bent leg out from beneath the other one and rose from the bed. She took one step away from the bed and, gazing deep into Yakima's eyes, reached up with one hand, pulled the towel free from her bosom, held it out to one side with aplomb, and let it drop.

She reached up and unpinned her hair. It tumbled in rich, auburn cascades about her shoulders and breasts, messily framing her face with its mysterious gray eyes, fine delicate nose, and warm sensuous lips. Again, a smile tugged at the corners of her mouth, and a playful light sparked in her eyes as, holding her arms half out to her sides, she turned a slow circle, so that he could feast his hungry eyes on every inch of her pale, beautiful body.

Finally, she stood facing him once more, her large, firm breasts up-tilted and swollen, nipples pebbling.

She slowly lowered her gaze from his eyes to just beyond his belly again, and then returned it to his eyes. "You like what you see, Marshal Henry," she said, huskily. It wasn't a question but a statement of fact.

Yakima swallowed down a tightness in his throat. His heart beat slowly but heavily against his breastbone. "Oh, yeah."

Remembering that he was covered in soap, he lowered himself into the water. Quickly, he rinsed off, squeezed water from his face with his hands, then rose once more to stand facing her in the tub. She'd moved up to him and stood not a foot away. She leaned forward and kissed him hungrily. Yakima placed his hand on her shoulders and drew her tighter against him.

"I missed you," he said, sliding her face away from his.

She smiled and averted her gaze shyly, showing the tips of her white front teeth beneath her plump upper lip. Slowly, she lifted her gaze to his once more. As she did, she bent her knees and dropped just as slowly to the floor, running her tongue down between the twin slabs of his chest, down over his iron-hard belly... down...

touching the tip of her tongue to the end of his almost painfully jutting cock.

She slid her tongue down the underside of the swollen mast until she was on her knees before him, gently cupping his balls in her hands, licking him, sucking...

When he could stand it no longer, he placed his hands on her shoulders, drew her to her feet, stepped out of the tub, took her hand, and led her over to the bed.

She rose onto her toes again and kissed him, smoothed his long, wet hair back behind his ears, then gave him a coquettish smile and crawled into bed, throwing the covers back. She spread herself out before him, extending her arms, reaching for him, a desperate cast of carnal desire making her eyes glisten.

Yakima crawled into the bed. He positioned himself between her legs. He pressed himself flat against her, feeling his staff pressing firmly against the triangle of hair between her thighs. It was warm and wet with desire. He lowered his head to hers, and they kissed tenderly, playfully, hungrily for a long time.

Groaning, she spread her legs and looked up at him, her eyes bright now with an even greater need than before.

"Oh, Yakima," she whispered in his ear as he slid his full length inside her. "Oh... oh... Yakima... you do know how to send me," she said in his ear.

She nibbled his lobe, then groaned as he pulled out

of her, to the very edge of her portal, then slid back inside her—slowly, tenderly, enjoying every moment of their union.

**

When Yakima and Julia had finished making love, they snoozed for a time, entangled in each other's arms and legs. Yakima woke with a start, hearing gunfire beyond the bedroom's open window.

"Oh, no!" Julia said, lifting her head from her pillow.

Yakima sat up and turned to the window, listening intently. There were two more gunshots, neither one close. A man whooped victoriously, and a horse whinnied. Julia wrapped an arm around her lover's waist, drawing herself taut against him. Beyond the window, from the direction of the town's center, another man bellowed an angry roar.

Yakima let out the breath he'd been holding and smiled. He turned to Julia, pressed his lips to her forehead. "Just some drunk drover popping some caps. That last shout was the Kid. He'll take care of it."

Such commotion before sundown was growing more and more common in Apache Springs.

Still, Julia shuddered against Yakima. "I hate that sound. It reminds me of…"

"Wilkes?"

She nodded.

"Don't worry." Yakima ran his hand up and down her back, nuzzled her neck. "Wilkes is dead. Nothing like that will ever happen again. Not here. At least, not as long as I'm here. I promise you."

He continued to nuzzle her neck, rubbing her back with his right hand while massaging her breasts with his left. They were warm and supple, swollen with desire.

"You're wonderful—you know that?" Her hand had found his manhood, and she was playing with it, bringing him to life again.

"Because I killed Wilkes?"

"No." She was growing breathless with desire, moving her hand faster. "Because… of… what you do to me… here… in bed."

"Oh."

"But also, because you killed Wilkes, that wretched bastard!" She threw her head back and squeezed her eyes closed, laughing throatily. Sometimes, in bed, when her guard was down, she reminded him of her more rustic, younger sister, though he shoved that bit of uncomfortable reflection to the back of his mind just now.

Yakima pushed her back down on the bed and made love to her once more.

When they were finished, they lay sweating together,

hot from their toil as well as from the furnace-like desert air pushing in through the open window. The sun was angling into the room, laying a trapezoid of yellow-gold light across their sprawled bodies—his large and brown body, her delicate, white one, both glistening with sweat.

Yakima gave a long, luxurious yawn, his desire sated, a pleasing dolor settling over him. He wanted to lie here forever, but, judging by the angle of the light, it was probably nearly five o'clock. He wanted to talk to Señora Galvez.

"I'd best be goin'."

But he didn't move. He just lay there, staring up at the bed's canopy. He found himself feeling very much at home in this bed. Julia rested her head on his chest and was brushing her fingers over the hard slab of his left pectoral and slowly sliding her right leg up and down his thigh.

He dropped his chin to glance down at her. Her eyes were pensive.

"What're you thinking about?"

She rolled her eyes up toward his, and a Y formed in the skin above the bridge of her nose. "Why the back door, Yakima?"

He sighed. "I'm a back-door kinda fella."

She lifted her head to level a direct look at him, her gray eyes penetrating. "Next time, use the front door."

"I don't think that—"

"Yakima"—she sat up and slid her face up to within a foot of his, sandwiching his own face in her hands—"I don't care what anybody thinks. And you shouldn't, either."

"I just don't want them to be hard on you. It can happen if we're not careful. You'll see."

"I don't care."

He placed his hands on her shoulders and returned her gaze with a sincere one of his own. "You will care, Julia. People can be ring-tailed mean, even those you've known a long time and trust. So far, things have gone all right. The badge helps. But if the good citizens of Apache Springs know that I'm, uh… *seein'*… a white woman, and not just any white woman but the previous marshal's widow *and* the daughter of Hugh Kos—"

Julia cut him off by placing two fingers over his lips. "Yakima, they already know."

He frowned. "What?"

"They know. At least, some do. I know they know. I can tell."

Yakima took her wrist in his hand, squeezed it gently. "How can you tell?"

"By the looks I get when I'm uptown shopping. Occasionally, I'll catch someone eyeing me as though they didn't think I'd notice." She lifted her head, defiantly shook her hair back from her face. "It doesn't bother me."

"Shit." Yakima turned away, thoughtful, a cold burning

starting in the pit of his gut. He'd wanted to prevent such a thing. He hadn't wanted to expose Julia to the same sort of prejudice he himself had to deal with all too often. He was used to it. She wasn't, whatever brave face she wanted to put on it.

What had he been thinking? How long did he think he... they... would get away with it?

She placed a hand on his cheek, turned his face toward hers. "Yakima." She gazed deeply into his eyes and smiled reassuringly; her gray eyes fairly glowing in the bright western light from the window. "I don't care. It doesn't bother me. Don't you know why?"

His eyebrows furled. "Why?"

She paused, her gaze becoming even more penetrating. "Because I love you."

That set him back on his proverbial heels. He wasn't sure how to respond. *Love.*

Why had he become so afraid of the word? He hadn't realized it, but he had. What horrible torment that one simple word could cause. Torment of so many different kinds.

"Well?" Julia said, narrowing her eyes slightly, probingly. "What do you have to say to *that,* Marshal Henry?"

Yakima looked away again. "You shouldn't."

"Why?"

"Because you shouldn't, Julia. I didn't realize it until

just now… until you said it." Yakima turned away from her, dropped one foot to the floor. She grabbed his arm, turned him back to face her. "You're not going anywhere. We're not going to leave it like this!"

He placed a hand gently along her jaw, caressed her delicate cheek with his thumb. "Julia, life could get tough. Very tough for you if we—"

She placed her hand on his hand caressing her cheek. "My father is taking care of me. I mean, if it's money you're worried about. How I'm able to support myself. My father stayed out of my life when I was married to Lon. But, now, with Lon dead… and all that happened… he's paid me a few visits and offered help in keeping me here in Apache Springs. In this house. He paid it off, in fact. He's even offered to hire me to keep his books over at the mercantile. He's expanding his business here in Apache Springs, investing in several different ventures, and he needs all the help he can get. I used to do his books for him, before…"

Before Taggart, too lowly for her father's approval, married her and brought her to town and Hugh Kosgrove all but disowned her.

Julia glanced away, as though searching for the words to express what was on her mind. She turned back to Yakima, her eyes resolute. "You make me very happy, Yakima Henry." She smiled and wrapped her arms around his neck, brushed her nipples against his chest. "Very happy, indeed."

She kissed his nose. "I love you. There. I said it again. I love you. A third time!" She dipped her chin and shaped a teasing smile. "Are you going to shame a girl for loving you?"

He gazed back at her.

Love.

What the hell?

There were worse words, he supposed. Worse ways to feel.

Ride it out, he told himself. Ride it out, see where it leads. It might surprise you. You might surprise yourself. It happened once. It might happen again. No need to worry about tomorrow.

Besides, can't you see how happy you—you damned badge-toting, half-breed, drifting fool—have made this woman after all she, like you, has lost?

Suddenly, he felt as though he were teetering atop the razor edge of a tall precipice. Afraid to move forward. Even more afraid to walk away. The room swirled around him. Life offered so few second chances, after all.

And here was one smiling at him now.

"I love you, Julia."

He wrapped his arms around her and kissed her, and they sagged back into the bed together once more.

Later, as long shadows striped the town of Apache Springs, Yakima stepped through Julia's front door and out onto her gallery. He drew the door closed behind him, latching it quietly.

He turned to face the street beyond her yard, beyond the gate in her whitewashed picket fence, abutted on each side by palo verdes. He felt uneasy. The back door, the whole backside of the house, concealed from possible watchers, beckoned him.

He fought off the impulse to turn around and walk back through the house, to head for the concealment of the wash. He moved to the edge of the gallery's steps. A steely resolve tightened inside him. There was no damned reason he should use the back door. She loved him. He loved her. Anyone who didn't like it could go to hell.

He dragged his makings sack out of his shirt pocket

and took his time rolling a smoke, standing there on Julia's front gallery, facing the street. He felt good, he realized. Better than he'd felt in a long time. It hadn't come from the mattress dance alone. True, there was nothing like a hot frolic in the proverbial hay with a beautiful woman, but he could get that at Señora Galvez's place, if he wanted to.

There was a lightness in him. A tenderness. The world didn't look as cold, harsh, and unfamiliar as it so often had in the past. His own life didn't feel so desperate.

Love.

Feeling sheepish, but then again not so sheepish... feeling good and light on his feet and at home here in Apache Springs... finally at home somewhere... he scratched a lucifer to life on the buckle of his shell belt and touched the flame to the quirley drooping from between his lips curved in a rare, sappy smile. He blew out the match with a puff of exhaled smoke, flipped it into the dust, and headed toward the gate.

Halfway through the small front yard, he turned to look up at a second-story window.

She stood there, waving, just as he knew she would be.

He chuckled and waved, then turned and opened the gate and stepped through it. When he'd drawn the gate closed behind him, he turned to the street. Two older women were just then walking along the avenue's far side, heading in the direction of Main Street. Both women, gray-haired and dressed in the wan colors and poke bonnets of their aproned lot, one bespectacled, gave him the wooly eyeball as they passed.

Yakima pinched his hat brim to the women and smiled. "Good afternoon, ladies!"

They turned abruptly away and continued walking, one leaning toward the other one, whispering. The disapproving biddies didn't bother Yakima. He had something they likely did not.

Whistling softly, feeling as light as an unabashed schoolboy in love, he followed the two biddies to Main Street, then hung a right and continued west toward Señora Galvez's place, identified by a single, understated sign under the gallery's front eave announcing simply, *SEÑORA GALVEZ.* The sign was enhanced by the red lamp burning in the white-curtained window to the right of the door. As Yakima started up the gallery's steps, he thought that above the horse and wagon traffic behind him he could hear a commotion inside—someone stomping around, girls gasping and yelling.

Inside, another, louder sound rose above the others—a man's enraged bellow.

Yakima hurried across the gallery and was reaching for the door when it opened suddenly. Señora Galvez stood in the doorway, copper-brown eyes flashing alarm.

"*¡Mierda!*" she said in surprise, stepping back in shock at the big half-breed standing before her, placing one hand on her heavy breast clad in several layers of silk and lace.

Alfonsina Galvez had a long, black wooden cigarette holder in her beringed right hand, and the air around her was rife with the peppery aroma of Mexican tobacco. "I was just going to send someone to fetch you. It's dire. Such animals!" She turned to yell up the stairs rising just inside the foyer, against its left wall. "*¡Bastardos! Pigs!* What have I told you about fighting in my place?"

The commotion was coming from the second story—men's shouting, heavy foot thuds. A fight.

"I'll handle it." Yakima brushed past the madam and headed up the stairs, taking the carpeted steps two at a time. Several girls, most half-dressed in underwear and light, colored wraps, ribbons in their hair, had gathered at the near end of the second-floor hall, and they were spilling onto the landing, all looking anxious as they stared down the hall to their right.

"Excuse me, ladies," Yakima said, nudging one of the frightened doxies aside as he stepped into the hall.

Ahead were two men. One was dressed only in long handles. He was the bigger of the two, but they were both big men. Yakima recognized the long-handle-clad gent as a crew chief for the spur line laying rails south of Apache Springs, connecting the town with the Southern Pacific line.

This was Mordicai Gunnison—a big, red-haired, red-bearded Irishman with a swirl of garish tattoos on his thick neck. The second man was Jim Halsey, a big, black-haired, black-bearded Scot freighter working for Nordstrom's Freighting out of Tucson, which had just opened an office in Apache Springs. They'd been contracted to haul ties for the spur line. Halsey wore shabby, dusty fringed buckskins, a hickory shirt, and suspenders, his shirtsleeves rolled up his muscular, brown forearms. A black bowler lay on the floor near his feet.

Both men had knives in their hands, and they were skirmishing, slashing at each other in the middle of the narrow hall, circling one another and cursing loudly. The Irishman called the Scot a dog-fucking son of a bitch, and the big Scot jerked his head forward to spit in Gunnison's face.

That enraged Gunnison even more, who brushed a big hand down his cheek and lunged at his opponent once more, the savage-looking blade of the big Bowie slashing through the air before Halsey, causing the big Scot to leap back with a startled grunt.

The Irishman's blade had sliced across Halsey's shirt, showing a thin line of red. "Bloody bastard!" the Scot roared. "I'm gonna gut you dirty for that one, ya ugly mick—and choke ya with your own entrails!"

"That's enough now, fellas," Yakima said, moving forward. "Put the blades away and play nice, or I'm going to take you both over to the lockup!"

"Stay out of this, breed!" yelled Gunnison, keeping his eyes on his opponent, who'd recovered enough that he was parrying with his adversary once more, both men lunging forward to slash, then jerking back to avoid their opponent's slicing blade.

"What the hell's this about?" Yakima asked, continuing to walk slowly forward.

"None o' your business, breed!" Halsey made another swipe at Gunnison's belly, nipping a button from the front of the man's balbriggan top.

One of the girls behind Yakima said loudly enough to be heard above the men's stomping feet, grunts, and curses, "Halsey doesn't want the mick screwin' Kansas Kate!"

"I done warned him," Halsey bellowed, making another slash at Gunnison—this one aimed for the Irishman's throat. "I don't want him stickin' his slimy Irish dick in my gal!"

"I ain't your gal, Jim!" a girl who was obviously Kansas Kate screamed furiously behind Yakima. Her voice owned a definite Southern lilt. "I done told you that! I ain't givin' neither one of you two shit heels a poke ever again! I done had it with the both of you privy-skulkin' varmints!"

Halsey wheeled toward Yakima but cast his gaze toward the girls huddled on the landing behind him. "Why, you sassy little—*achhh-ohhhh, jayzuzzz*!"

Yakima had just stepped forward to kick the knife out of the man's clenched fist. The Bowie flew straight up to bounce off the ceiling before hitting the hall floor in front of Halsey, who grabbed his right wrist with his left hand and bellowed, crouching against the wall to Yakima's right.

"Ohhhh, sweet merciful Jesus—the fuckin' Injun done broke my wrist!"

Yakima had seen Gunnison, crouched low and grinning devilishly, lunge forward, jabbing his own Bowie toward Yakima's belly. Ready for it, the lawman jerked back and sideways. The Irishman grunted, then stumbled forward, propelled past Yakima by his own momentum. When he was just beyond Yakima's right shoulder, Yakima chopped his own hand down hard against the back of the man's neck.

The Irishman bellowed, legs buckling, knees hitting the floor with a thunderous boom. He tried reaching for the knife. Yakima delivered two powerful left jabs to the man's right ear. Gunnison's head slammed against the wall.

He froze for a moment, on his knees, eyes rolling up

in their sockets. Slowly, his arms sagged, and he leaned forward. He gave a shrill sigh, as though he'd suddenly become deeply tired, and crumpled like a pile of dirty laundry, out like a light.

"You red-skinned son of a bitch!" This from the Scottish freighter, Halsey, still holding his right wrist, which was cast at an odd angle and had a nasty-looking lump in it, with his left hand. He knelt on the other side of Gunnison. His big, bearded face was a mask of red fury, molasses-dark eyes sparking flames. "You broke my fuckin' wrist! I can't skin a team without my wrist!"

Yakima turned to him and pitched his voice with soft menace. "If you don't stop your caterwauling, Jim, I'm gonna break the other wrist and shove both hands so far up your ass you'll be able to scratch your tonsils!"

One of the girls behind Yakima muffled a laugh with her hand.

Another voice—this one a man's—said, "Well, I was just gonna ask you if you needed any assistance, but..."

Yakima turned to see the Rio Grande Kid standing behind him, holding his long-barreled, double-bore Greener up high across his broad chest and staring down at the two fighters—one out like a blown lamp, the other on his knees, glaring and gritting his teeth at the half-breed lawman. Yakima saw that Galveston Penny had come with the Kid, both deputies probably having heard reports of violence at Señora Galvez's place through word on the street.

Young Penny stood on the landing behind the Kid, his hat in his hands. He was grinning like a coyote with a mouth full of cockleburs as he chatted with a small, plump, Mexican girl with a heart-shaped face and wearing a little pink corset under a powder-blue wrap as thin as a butterfly's wing, and not a whole lot else.

Señorita Clara—barefoot, her hair in braids—smiled coquettishly up at young Penny, who was a good head taller than the comely young *puta*. The pair could have been on a separate planet, for all the awareness either seemed to have of the dustup that had just occurred a mere ten feet beyond the landing.

Yakima loudly cleared his throat and said, "Excuse me, Casanova."

He had to say it two more times, each time a little louder, before Penny finally looked at him, his face and ears suddenly turning crimson. He bounded forward and said, "You callin' me, Marshal?"

"If you're not too busy, I was wondering if you could help the Kid cart this brainless sack of Irish shit out to the street. Dump some water on him. When he wakes up, make sure he understands that he's been banned from town for two months."

Yakima glanced at Halsey. "That goes for you, too, Jim.

If I see either of you two chuckleheads in town within two months, you're gonna be spending that long in the lockup—when I don't have you volunteering your time mucking out stalls in one of the livery barns, I mean."

Halsey hauled himself to his feet and, grimacing over the broken wrist he held against his chest like an injured sparrow, stumbled up to Yakima. Keeping his voice low, but hard with menace, he said, "I'm gonna kill you for this." He winked. "You can put money on that… *breed*!"

He'd shoved his face up close to Yakima's before spewing that last.

Yakima smiled. Then he drew his right arm back and shot it forward, plunging his clenched fist deep into the Scot's midsection. Halsey jackknifed, his wind gushing out of him with the ferocity of a cyclone, and hit the floor again on his knees.

"You can't say I didn't warn you not to try, Jim."

"Ohhh!" Halsey cried, bowing his head as though genuflecting in church. *"Ohhhh!"*

The Kid, working a wad of chaw around in his mouth, stepped up beside Yakima. "Want I should lock this one up, boss?" He stared down at the miserably groaning Scot.

"Might be a good idea. Keep an eye on him, you know." He looked at Yakima, then leaned toward him and said quietly, "Or take him south of town an' blow his head off? Give him a *proper* burial?"

He smiled deviously, sucking the chaw against his gums.

"No need," Yakima said. "I think Jim got the message."

Señora Galvez had been watching the hall's festivities from the landing with her girls. Now, wielding her cigarette holder like a weapon, she walked up beside Yakima, and, holding a lacy cape about her otherwise bare, freckled shoulders, glared down at the burly Scot. "The marshal might have only barred you from town for two months, Señor Halsey. But you are banned for life from these premises. *¿Comprende, amigo?*"

Halsey looked up at her, black eyes bright with rage. He opened his mouth to spout an ungentlemanly retort, but then he saw Yakima staring down with a menacing half smile, and he merely gritted his teeth and averted his gaze.

"Out!" the Kid yelled at the Scot, stepping back and clicking his Greener's hammers back. "Before I revert to my old outlaw ways!"

When the Kid had shepherded Halsey down the stairs and he and Galveston Penny had carried the still-unconscious Gunnison down the stairs and onto the gallery, Señora Galvez turned to Yakima, removing the cigarette holder from her painted mouth and blowing smoke toward the ceiling.

She looked the half-breed lawman up and down speculatively, taking his measure, and said, "I would warn another man to watch his back. Halsey is a killer. He might skin mules for a living, but on the side he's a killer. I should have banned him long ago."

"What do you mean you'd warn another man?"

"You can take care of yourself just fine." She drew on the cigarette holder again and crooked the other half of her mouth with approval. Her gaze fell to Yakima's hand hanging at his side. "Do you need something for that?"

Yakima lifted the hand and inspected the knuckles, some of the skin of which he must have left on Halsey's ear. Before he could respond, a young blonde with henna-rinsed hair stepped forward, extending a length of white flannel. She wore only a thin chemise—so thin that it made her small, pert breasts appear all but bare.

"Here," she said. "And… thanks, Marshal."

Yakima accepted the cloth. "Kansas Kate?"

The girl nodded, smiled. She was tall and slender and rather plain-faced, but there was an attractive earthiness in her pale-blue eyes. A pale, white scar curved down over her jaw on the right side of her face, two inches in front of her ear.

"He won't be back," Yakima said, wrapping the cloth around his hand. "I'll see to it."

"Like I said," Kansas Kate said, shaking her hair back from her cheeks, which had colored a little, "thanks."

"You can go, now, Kate," Señora Galvez said crisply

and blew another plume of smoke toward the ceiling. "The marshal and I have something to discuss."

Kansas Kate smiled at Yakima once more, then turned, let the strap of her chemise tumble off her shoulder, and flounced away down the hall and into a near room, casting one more coy look back at the big lawman before closing and latching her door.

When Yakima and the Mexican madam were standing alone in the hall, Señora Galvez said, "You can have her for free if you like. For what you did here today and for the two you hauled in dead. I'll give you two hours. You can do what you like, just don't leave any bruises. I have trouble getting girls way out here, even more trouble keeping them."

Yakima shrugged, shook his head. "Not necessary."

Señora Galvez frowned as she studied him probingly. "Is it the scar?"

"Hell, no. I got plenty of those myself."

"What, then?"

Yakima put some authoritative steel in his voice as he said, "Let's just say it's not necessary, Señora Galvez, and leave it at that."

"All right." The madam smiled a little woodenly, looking him up and down once more, obviously puzzled.

Señora Galvez was a woman who liked to get a firm handle on those around her, to know who or what they were exactly, probably so that she could manipulate them when needed. She wasn't pleased when Yakima's handle didn't come as easily as she would have liked.

"Have it your way, big man," she said with more than a little frustration. "Can I buy you a drink?"

"I'd take a beer."

She arched a brow, again taken aback by the man before her. "Just beer?"

"The firewater turns me into Halsey," Yakima said with a wry smile.

"*¡Cristos!*" Señora Galvez laughed, then turned and beckoned with her smoldering cigarette holder. "Come!"

10

Yakima followed the madam along the whorehouse's third-floor hall, her tail wind rife with the smell of peppery Mexican tobacco and a not overly cloying perfume.

The half-breed wasn't an authority on fragrances, but he had a feeling what he was smelling now wasn't the cheap sort sold for a dollar or two a bottle at the mercantile. This, like the freight wagons that had pulled up to the whorehouse not long after the last shake shingle was nailed to its roof, its paint still drying on its clapboard siding, had probably come from Mexico City, which was from where the madam was rumored to hail.

Señora Galvez was also rumored to be a refugee of a scandal of some sort, likely involving powerful men in the Mexican government. Very little bonded fact was known about Señora Galvez beyond that her opulent furnishings had been shipped from Mexico City, and that the madam herself had followed them a week later in a fine carriage guarded by dusky-skinned, mustachioed Mexican men dressed in wagon wheel *sombreros,* brightly colored and ruffle-fronted *camisas,* bell-bottomed and elaborately embroidered *charro* slacks, and short leather jackets. Her *caballero* entourage had also been heavily armed.

Her men had lingered in town for a few days, presumably helping the madam settle in to her new abode. They left early one morning before anyone else in Apache Springs had been out and about. Aside from its newly reappointed town marshal, that is…

A door opened ahead of the madam, and a girl came out of a room, stretching sleepily. She was a young, tall, impossibly slender Mexican with vaguely Indio features and long, coarse black hair, some of which was braided with strips of dyed rawhide. Señora Galvez grabbed the girl's arm and said in rapid Spanish, "Eva, summon Clara, *por favor.* Tell her to fetch a bottle of cool ale from the springhouse and come to my office *pronto.*"

"Si, si, Señora," said Eva, all painted up and decked out in a pink corset and black and silver bustier for the night ahead. Sleep lines from a pillow remained in her otherwise smooth, dark-brown cheeks.

In passing, she gave Yakima a long, slow blink with her muddy eyes and brushed the very tips of her fingers across his arm, smiling devilishly and flouncing off down the hall.

"Eva, don't act like a child!" the madam admonished the girl, who was already on the stairs, chuckling throatily.

The madam sighed and threw open the door at the end of the hall, on the hall's left side.

"They are like herding cats, these girls. *Por favor,*" she said, extending an arm to indicate the small but nicely appointed office before her. "There is some dust, but I can't find a girl who cleans to my preferences. They are barbarians, mostly. Nothing like the girls in the city. Have a seat."

Yakima approached a leather armchair angled in front of a leather-topped desk adorned with a pink lamp that resembled an exotic, long-legged water bird. Likely shipped all the way to the Sierra Estrada from Mexico City.

"No," the madam said, brusquely. "Not there. There." She indicated a short, red velvet sofa fronting a cold, brick fireplace and a small table topped with a cut-glass decanter and two brandy snifters atop a polished silver tray.

Yakima considered the sofa, shrugged, and doffed his hat. He walked over and sagged into the sofa, angling toward Señora Galvez as she took a seat beside him, on the sofa's other end. She gazed at him with a vague curiosity as she drew on her cigarette holder, making the tip of the cigarette glow.

She was an amazingly beautiful woman, Yakima saw

now, in the light of two large windows facing them. She was probably in her late thirties or early forties, judging by the crows' feet around her almond-shaped, light-brown eyes, and around her plump-lipped mouth.

Her cheeks were still firm and smooth, the color of varnished walnut. Her lashes were long and dark. Yakima had never been this close to the madam—in fact, he'd only seen her from a distance a handful of times in all the months she'd been in town—but he saw now that she had at one time been ravishing and was still beautiful. Handsome, he supposed is what most would call her now. He himself would still call her right fetching.

No wonder she'd gotten in trouble with the rich and powerful in Mexico. A woman as beautiful as the one before him could cause quite a war down south of the border.

"What's funny?"

Yakima hadn't realized he'd been smiling.

"Oh, uh… nothing."

She smiled with faint, good-humored sarcasm and poked the cigarette holder between her rich, bee-stung lips once more, drawing deeply, then holding her breath. "Share your thoughts with me, Marshal," she urged, letting smoke trickle out her nostrils.

"I was considering the rumors about you. Stacking them up beside the woman I see now."

"Rumors, eh?"

"Sure."

"And who is the woman you see... just out of friendly curiosity?"

"A most beautiful one, Señora Galvez."

She turned her head slightly to one side, smiling with one half of her mouth, skeptically. "Are you flirting with me, Marshal Henry?"

"Not at all, Señora. You asked me what I was thinking, and I told you. You're a beautiful woman. A mysterious one."

"I see. Well, do you know that you are shrouded in your own cloud of rumors, uh... what was your first name again?"

"Yakima."

"Yakima. Interesting. Indio, I take it."

"Half."

"I see." She frowned again as she nibbled the end of her cigarette holder. "Don't you want to know what the girls say about you?"

"The girls?"

"The girls in my employ. Oh, they are quite interested in the handsome, Indio town marshal. They watch from the balconies, muttering among themselves like lovelorn schoolgirls. Few have seen a red man wearing a badge. They are partly fearful, remembering the Apache

123

depredations of recent history—some of my girls were orphaned by the *Coyoteros*—and partly attracted. *Intrigado,* I guess would be the right word. Intrigued."

Yakima chuffed with self-deprecation. "I won't spoil the mystery for them."

"They'd love to have it spoiled. In their beds, of course. They get tired of the more common fare around here." She flipped a hand, lit with several sparkling rings, toward a window, indicating the town beyond.

She smiled more broadly, showing her fine, white teeth, brown eyes flashing more than a little coquettishly. Still, Yakima didn't think she was flirting with him. Maybe building an alliance? Against what or whom, he didn't know. He had a feeling the mysterious, beautiful Mexican madam was in the habit, shaped by necessity, of building allegiances.

"How come I never see you over here, Marshal? You might wear a badge, but you're still a man... with a man's needs. I certainly don't take you for a Nancy-boy."

Yakima chuckled. "No. Nothin' like that. Frankly, Señora, I'm just too damn busy to think about it all that much."

"How terrible for you!" She feigned a pout, pooching out her erotic lips. "Anytime you want, I'll stake you to a couple of free hours with the girl of your choice. Any time at all, Marshal Henry." She held his gaze, continuing to probe him, her curiosity about him fairly boiling over inside her.

He had to admit feeling more than a little curious about the madam, but she owned the air of a woman who held her own cloak of secrecy very closely about her shoulders. He was only mildly curious, anyway. He had enough to worry about in the here and now in Apache Springs.

"I'll keep that in mind, Señora," Yakima said. "But I'll probably be passin' on it, just the same." Julia was enough for him.

A knock came at the door.

Señora Galvez winced slightly, as though she wasn't ready for their conversation to be over just yet. As though there was more she wanted to know about Apache Springs's half-breed marshal. Or maybe there was more that she wanted to discuss.

Fatefully, she sighed. "That will be Clara." She turned to yell behind her, "Come, Clara!"

The door latch clicked, and the door opened. The pretty little Mexican girl—the apple of Galveston Penny's eye—came in holding a tray a little uncertainly before her, a beer bottle wobbling atop the tray. Clara chewed her lower lip with concentration. The young *puta* was dressed for the night ahead in an intoxicating black velvet negligee that dipped so low in front that it covered only the tips of her small, tan breasts. The girl wore a small, black, velvet box cap pinned at an angle atop her head. The cap was adorned with a black velvet bow. Dark-brown braids trailed down over her shoulders.

Several strands of *faux* pearl necklaces hung down her chest. Her brown legs were bare between long, black, sheer stockings that rose to just above her knees, held in place with a red velvet and black garter belt, and a pair of very short, red lace bloomers edged in silver.

On her feet were black satin shoes with pointed toes and three-inch square heels, black buttons running down the insides.

Yakima felt a pang of chagrin at the male heat rising in him as the girl walked past him, nearly stumbling over her own shoes, and leaned down to set the tray on the table. The negligee dipped away from her chest, giving him a complete picture of her tender, brown-nippled breasts. Her necklaces swung down and would have tipped the beer bottle she was trying to balance on the tray if Yakima hadn't reached forward to catch it.

The *senorita,* dolled up to entice the gentlemen of Apache Springs, had the air of a small girl playing dress up. A small girl filling out nicely, however. There it was again—the twinge of lust in the half-breed's denims. His ear tips warmed in shame. Now he saw up close what had so attracted Galveston Penny to the pretty little *senorita* whose sensitive eyes betrayed a tender heart.

Penny likely had the urge to take her away from all this.

"Oh, Clara, *please,*" admonished the madam. "I have shown you girls so many times how to set down a tray." She glanced at Yakima. "See what I mean? Barbarians!"

"¡Lo siento, Señora!" the girl cried, straightening and covering her breasts with the tray. "You wanted to see me?" she continued in Spanish, glancing a little shyly at Yakima as she stepped back toward the cold fireplace climbing the wall behind her.

"*Si, si*—I did not summon you to show off your serving skills." Señora Galvez had plucked a ready-made cigarette from a wooden box on the table before her and was sticking it into her holder. "Go ahead—tell Marshal Henry what you overheard the two *gringos* discussing last night."

Clara shifted her eyes again to Yakima. "They thought I was asleep," she whispered. "When the one had finished with me, the other one came in and sat in a chair."

"Clara, speak up," the madam urged. "We can't hear you."

Yakima leaned forward, resting his elbows on his knees, and smiled reassuringly at the obviously anxious doxie. "It's all right. You're safe in here, *senorita.* What were these two *gringos* discussing?"

"A job of some kind," she said, clearing her throat and

squeezing the tray in her hands. "A hold-up job, I think. They didn't say that, but I could tell it was something like that. Something against the law."

Clara took an anxious step forward, staring down at Yakima. "*Senor,* er… Marshal Henry…" She swallowed, hesitating, squeezing the tray even harder in her small hands.

"Yes, *senorita,*" Yakima prodded gently, dipping his chin. "Continue."

"They were men from the fire. From the men who set the fire. Two years ago. Remember? These two were part of that bunch, and, from what I heard, I think there are more men from that gang in Apache Springs."

Yakima's heart quickened. Six from Wilkes's original gang of twelve hadn't been brought to justice. The bunch had split up out in the desert, and Yakima, the Rio Grande Kid, and Emma Kosgrove had gone after the bunch led by Wilkes, because Wilkes had kidnapped Julia. Yakima had assumed the six survivors had continued on to Mexico, where he'd figured they were still cooling their heels after burning the town.

"How do you know?" he asked the girl.

"From what they said about the fire. And… because I remembered one of them." Clara's voice lowered again, and she looked downward, eyes bright with remembered horror. "The one who lay with me last night."

A wetness glazed the girl's eyes. A tear rolled down her cheek. It tumbled off her chin and onto the toe of her left shoe. "I was working the line then, too. Here in Apache Springs… when they came to town that day. Two of them broke into Mrs. Fitzsimmons's house and shot some of the girls." Mrs. Fitzsimmons owned a brothel the gang had burned, killing the madam herself. "They savaged the girls. Raped them brutally, making them cry, making them scream! I hid under a bed upstairs and watched in horror. I will never forget that night. I remember the man who came to me last night from that night two years ago. He savaged a girl in front of me, in the room we shared, and cut her throat before my eyes."

Clara hardened her jaws and gritted her teeth, more tears rolling down her cheeks. "I was terrified when I saw him. I recognized him right away. He has very black hair. It waves down across his forehead." She brushed one of her own hands across her own forehead. "A black mustache, too. A thick one. But it is his eyes that stand out. They are the deepest, darkest blue I have ever seen. There is no good in them. No good at all. Do you know what I mean?"

"I know what you mean."

"When he finished with me last night, I pretended to fall asleep. In reality, I was terrified that he would cut my throat. He took a long time, and he was very angry by the end. He was dressing when the other one came in, a blond man with black *chaparreras*. He sat in a chair, and the blue-eyed man sat down on the bed, and while I feigned sleep, they shared a jug of whiskey and smoked and talked about the big job they had planned."

"But they weren't specific? They didn't say exactly what this big job was?"

"No." Again, Clara lowered her eyes to the floor and hesitated before adding, "But they said they had one important task before they did that job they were talking about."

"Did they say what that task was?"

Clara lifted her chin and looked at Yakima directly. "To kill you... the Indio lawman. They said they were looking forward to 'settling up for two years ago.' "

"Ah," Yakima said. They must have learned that the current town marshal, the badge-toting half-breed, had been one of the men who'd chased them into the desert two years ago and killed half their bunch, including Wilkes.

They were probably still chafed by that. And wanted revenge, as well as to get him out of their way.

What else did they want? What big job did they have planned?

"Is there anything else, Clara?" Señora Galvez asked the girl sharply. "Come, come—out with the rest. Don't let the cat get your tongue!"

The girl jerked, startled by the madam's own sharp tongue. She shook her head. "That is all."

"You didn't get their names?" Yakima asked. "The two men in your room?"

Clara furled her brows, thinking. "The blue-eyed man didn't tell me his name. But I heard him call the blond-haired man Les."

"Les?"

"*Si.*"

"All right, then," Yakima said. "I'm much obliged, Clara. If you happen to see either of them in town again, let me know, will you?"

"*Si,* I will." She glanced at the madam. "May I go, Señora?"

"*Si,* you're excused." Señora Galvez waved the smoldering cigarette holder at the door. "Go down and play the piano. That will calm your nerves."

"*Si.*" The girl walked to the door and went out.

Señora Galvez glanced at Yakima. "You'd better watch your back."

"I reckon," Yakima said with a sigh, rising. "I appreciate you letting me know about this, Señora." He started toward the door.

"You haven't even opened your beer. Why don't you stay a while, drink with me? A woman gets lonely in this big house with all these young women running about half-dressed, reminding her how old and ugly she's getting."

Yakima stopped at the door and turned back to the madam still sitting on the sofa, half-turned toward him. "Is that why you're so... so..." Yakima looked around as though searching for the right word. "So short with these girls? You resent their youth?"

She studied him from the sofa. Yakima saw a fiery light blaze in her light-brown eyes, but then it dwindled, and she said, "Being a man, you wouldn't understand what it's like being a woman. Being an aging woman."

"You're a beautiful woman, Señora."

"Gracias," she said automatically, as though the compliment were no real comfort.

Yakima studied her, turning his hat slowly in his hands. He considered what he'd heard about her relationship with Cleve Dundee, and then decided to go ahead and ask the impertinent question: "No man in your life?"

She shook her head, and suddenly her eyes, once ready to catch fire, betrayed a deep inner sorrow. "No man. At least, not in the way you mean." She turned her head forward and drew on the cigarette holder.

He thought that was a shame. He didn't know Señora Galvez very well, but he thought he could like her. And he knew how important it was to have someone in one's life. He couldn't help feeling at long last fortunate in that regard.

"Good night, Señora," Yakima said, setting his hat on his head.

"Oh, call me Alfonsina, won't you?" Glancing at him over her shoulder, she shaped a slow smile, adding. "Yakima…"

"Alfonsina it is. Good night and thanks."

"Good night, Yakima. Be careful out there. Wolves are on the prowl, and this town is getting wilder by the day."

Yakima opened the door and left the somber madam on her sofa, smoking, hearing the wolves yipping and snarling inside her own head.

Yakima went downstairs and stepped outside onto the small gallery fronting the whorehouse. He'd heard a deep rumbling while he was inside the house, and now he saw what was causing it.

One of Hugh Kosgrove's ore trains was pulling through town, heading from east to west along Main Street. The pass upon which Apache Springs sat was the only negotiable route from the Conquistador to the Southern Pacific line to the southwest. From there the ore would be transported via train to the smelter at Tucson. From the smelter, the ingots would be sent to the US Mint in San Francisco.

Soon, the spur line would transport the gold, but until the rails had been laid, Kosgrove had to move his ore via the large, mule-drawn ore drays now moving past Señora Galvez's place. The heavy-wheeled, stout-axled, high-sided Bascom wagons kicked up as much dust as a Texas twister. In fact, standing on the gallery, Yakima couldn't see much *except* the dust. He couldn't smell much of anything except the mules.

He could hear the mule skinners yelling at their six-hitch teams, hear the blacksnakes popping above the teams' backs and the thunderous clomping of the mules' shod hooves, as well as the noisy, squeaky clatter of the wagon wheels that were nearly as tall as Yakima himself. Vaguely and occasionally, he could see one of Kosgrove's heavily armed outriders trotting past in the roiling dust, a vague figure holding a rifle or shotgun on his shoulder or high across his chest, neckerchief drawn up over his mouth and nose.

Yakima knew that many of the town's inhabitants would welcome the day that Kosgrove's wagons no longer bisected Apache Springs. The townsfolk complained about the earthquake-like shaking and the din of the monstrous teams and wagons, and about the dust that sifted for nearly an hour after the last team and wagon had passed on out of town, after pausing for water at the springs at the town's edge. Two years ago, the town had preferred the ore trains passing through once every two or three weeks to the spur-line train that would likely come and go through the very heart of town at least twice weekly.

Now, with a mostly new population in the wake of the marauders' burning of the original town, the sentiment had changed. The new folks, mostly lured here by gold in the surrounding mountains, wanted the growth and prosperity a railroad would bring.

Yakima himself was wary. He'd seen what "prosperity" had done to other towns across the west. Then again, he'd found himself unexpectedly liking it here, though Julia Taggart had played no small part in that, and prosperity meant his job was reasonably secure. It was also nice to see folks living relatively happily and comfortably, and he liked being a part of such a community.

"You Henry?"

Yakima hadn't realized someone had ridden up to the gallery he was standing on. Now he saw the gent materializing from the swirling dust, holding a Colt revolving rifle across the bows of his saddle and tugging a red bandanna down beneath his chin. He was a tall, mustached man riding a high-stepping Arabian steeldust.

"I'm Henry."

"Jake Salko, foreman on Kosgrove's ore train." His horse was prancing around, excited by the commotion of the wagons and mules and other outriders moving behind him. "Mister Kosgrove wanted me to invite you out to the Conquistador tomorrow for noon dinner. Twelve sharp." He put some slack in his horse's reins, and the Arab bolted on down the street like grapeshot fired from a cannon, Salko calling over his shoulder, "Don't be late!"

"Invitation, huh?" Yakima said, mostly to himself, running a hand across his cheek and staring after Salko and the last of the five ore wagons rocking and thundering on out of town.

"Sounds more like an order to me."

Yakima turned to see the Kid walk around from the end of the gallery on Yakima's left and stop at the gallery's left corner, gazing after the ore train. Thick dust blocked the view in that direction.

"Yeah," Yakima said, thoughtful. "Me, too."

"You suppose he's got trouble out there?"

"I reckon I'll find out tomorrow."

As town marshal, Yakima's official jurisdiction ended at the edge of Apache Springs. But since the county sheriff was quartered in Tucson, sixty miles away, Yakima assumed the role of deputy sheriff when trouble beckoned from the far reaches of the county. The sheriff, Henry Stafford, had swung through Apache Springs to swear him in. The growing city of Tucson and its surrounding environs kept the portly, middle-aged sheriff and his deputies hopping; they had no time to investigate every rustled cow or jumped mine around Apache Springs. Such problems were up to Yakima and his own two deputy town marshals.

"Want me to ride out there with you?" the Kid asked, setting his Greener on his shoulder and squinting one eye at his boss. "That's trouble country. Outlaws hole up in them canyons between town and the Conquistador. Some renegade 'Paches, too. I know all too well. When I was lookin' for Eddie's treasure, a coupla them bronco 'Pache braves got the wrong idea that this old man would be an easy mark for his hoss and the change in his pockets."

The Kid spat to one side. "Let's just say they was wrong. They're snugglin' with the diamondbacks now for their foolishness." He ran a stout, freckled forearm across his mouth and grinned.

"Don't doubt it a bit," Yakima said. "But I need you here in town."

He told the Kid about what he'd learned from young Clara in Señora Galvez's office, about the two men who were likely survivors from Wilkes's gang of town-burning marauders.

"You don't say?" the Kid said in astonishment. "You know, I was wonderin' what became of the second half of that bunch."

"I figured they were in Mexico."

"I reckon I figured as much. What job you think they might be plannin'?"

"I got no idea. Maybe the bank. Maybe the Busted

Flush. Lord knows Dundee's got enough money movin' through his swing doors every day an' night. He'd be a tasty target."

"I'll tell him to keep his cash box locked."

"You do that. Inform Galveston. You both be on the lookout for that black-haired gent with the dead blue eyes and his sidekick, some blond-headed fella named Les." Yakima stepped down off the gallery's front steps and into the street, where the dust from the ore train was still sifting. "I'm gonna take a stroll around town, see what I can see. Then I'll head back to the office and make like I'm catching up on some of that consarned paperwork."

"Sounds good, boss," the Kid said. "But, say, about Eddie's treasure map…"

Yakima glanced over his shoulder at the older man. "Kid, didn't you hear what I just told you? We got more important things to worry about than Eddie's treasure map!"

Yakima quickened his step as he headed east along the main drag.

"All right," the Kid yelled behind him. "But we'll be powwowin' on that very topic soon enough, by Jim! This old outlaw don't cotton to claim jumpers!"

Yakima knew he could prolong the Kid's inquiry only so long. The old outlaw had a right to know about the treasure map. Yakima's predicament lay in how to tell the Kid about the missing map—or about how Yakima figured it was missing—without telling him about the canyon full of cursed Apache gold.

***

The next morning, at nearly midday, the sun straight up and nary a shadow anywhere around, the sun beating down to the rhythm of several hidden cicadas, Yakima reined Wolf to a halt on a low pass littered with boulders and saguaros as well as several other varieties of cactus and wiry desert shrub.

A few minutes ago, he'd started hearing a loud but distant din from dead ahead, issuing from a broad canyon between whose natural stone gates he was now. The din consisted of drumming and squawking sounds. The industrious cacophony told Yakima that he was nearing Hugh Kosgrove's Conquistador mine. As he'd continued to ride toward the canyon gaping before him, the sounds had quickly grown louder.

Now, sitting atop the low pass at the canyon's mouth, he stared off over a devil's playground of up-thrust rock and knife-slash arroyos to a distant sandstone and limestone ridge with a large black hole in it—the Conquistador itself.

Yakima had not been out here to these far reaches of

the Sierra Estrada, a good two-hour ride on a good horse from Apache Springs. He'd never had reason to ride this far into the high and rocky—no previous invitation to join Kosgrove for his midday meal or any other meal. In fact, while the half-breed lawman had seen Hugh Kosgrove in town more than a few times over the past months, now that the man was investing largely in several Apache Springs businesses, Yakima had never been formally introduced to the former eastern speculator and general mucky-muck turned Arizona mine owner.

And father of two lovely daughters, Yakima couldn't help reminding himself, though it wasn't something he was liable to forget, both young women having played fairly large roles in Yakima's life in that he'd slept with both of them. And had fallen in love with one.

He eased his mind away from that bit of unnecessary distraction and concentrated on the canyon before him.

He saw what was making the thundering, squawking sounds. Ore cars were being rolled out of the mine's black mouth onto what appeared to be a short trestle bridge sprouting from the side of the rocky cliff. The ore cars were rolled by hand by two or three men, little larger than ants from this distance, out to the end of the bridge and then upended.

The upending was what caused the squawking. The thundering sounds, owning several variations in pitch, were caused by the ore from the rail cars striking the giant wooden bin jutting from the shoulder of the mountain below the bridge. The thundering was also caused by the louvered steel doors of the ore cars slamming shut before being latched by one of the attending miners.

Then the cars were wheeled back into the mine on a separate return track for another load of gold-rich ore.

"Damned hot, dirty, bone-grinding job," Yakima muttered to himself now.

He knew that for a fact, for he'd worked for such a mine a time or two, for as long as he could take it, which hadn't been long.

He'd just touched Wolf with his spurs to start down the far side of the pass, following a trail cut deep by the shod rims of many ore wagons, when he pulled back on the reins again sharply. Hooves thudded, growing quickly louder. Two horseback riders were approaching at a fast clip.

He could see them converging on the main trail from about fifty yards ahead and to either side of the trail. Mostly, he could see dust and brief glimpses of the riders' hats as they raced over the harsh, broken terrain.

Both riders converged on the main trail and continued toward Yakima before galloping around a sharp bend in the trail, dashing out from behind a bulging belly of white rock, and reining their own mounts to skidding halts.

Both men carried rifles.

The man on the left took his Winchester in both hands, loudly cocked it, glared toward Yakima sitting atop the pass, and yelled, "Who in the hell are you, and what in the hell do you want?" He lowered the rifle, aiming the black maw at the newcomer. "Make it fast or swallow lead!"

Yakima gave a wry snort. The poetic gent had been reading too many dime novels for his own good.

"Get the hump out of your necks. I'm Yakima Henry. *Marshal* Yakima Henry from Apache Springs. I was given a dance card."

The rider not aiming the rifle at Yakima leaned toward the one who was and whispered something. They were obviously mine guards, probably two of many keeping a close eye on this canyon. When the second man stopped whispering, the first one raised his rifle and depressed the hammer.

"Well, why in the hell didn't you say so? Come on!"

Both guards reined their horses around and headed straight off down the trail.

"Some folks were just born with burs under their blankets," Yakima muttered as he put Wolf into a trot behind Kosgrove's men.

Yakima galloped Wolf into the dust of his two-man, rifle-wielding welcoming committee.

They passed a broad, deeply rutted trail that obviously led off toward the rocky ridge wall and the mine and continued along the main trail that followed a broad wash, before swerving sharply left and climbing up and out of the wash and into another, secondary canyon fingering off from the main one. The riders climbed a broad, low bench and then another, even higher, bench. Spreading out across the bench before him, Yakima saw what appeared to be a Mexican *hacienda* complete with brightly whitewashed adobe barns, stables, and pole corrals, including a round stone breaking corral with a snubbing post at its center.

Last, but certainly not least, a sprawling, low, Spanish-style *casa* hunched behind a six-foot-high whitewashed adobe wall boasting a broad, wrought-iron gate with the name *KOSGROVE* fashioned of wrought iron in the gate's center.

The house fronted the barns and other outbuildings, quartering off to the right and flanked by a steeply slanted mesa wall shimmering in the midday heat haze. There was a veritable orchard of what appeared to be lemon and orange trees and maybe a few nut trees behind the wall. The trees spread welcoming shade over a courtyard patio.

Yakima and his chaperones reined up before the gate.

The man who'd done all the talking a few minutes ago now turned his frisky grullo gelding back toward Yakima and said in a habitually sneering voice, "We'll corral your horse. Just hang your pistol belt from the horn."

Yakima looked at him.

The man smiled without an ounce of humor. "Kosgrove house rules. No visitors with weapons get through that gate."

Yakima gave a caustic snort. It wasn't like he'd invited himself out here. And he certainly wasn't here to assassinate Hugh Kosgrove. But he was here now, and he had a feeling arguing his point wouldn't do him much good. Besides, Wolf needed water and rest before making the long, hot ride back to Apache Springs.

Yakima swung down from the saddle, tossed his reins to the ill-tempered gent, removed his holstered Colt and cartridge belt, buckled the rig, and hooked it over his saddlehorn.

"Enjoy your meal, Marshal Henry," the ill-tempered gent said in his ill-tempered tone, accentuating "marshal." He obviously didn't think a man with Yakima's skin tone should be wearing a badge.

"If I enjoy it even half as much as your company, I'll have a leg up on the rest of the day."

The ill-tempered gent's partner laughed at that. He looked at the ill-tempered gent, who wasn't smiling, so his partner tugged his hat brim low, obliterating his own smile.

Leading Wolf by his bridle reins, the ill-tempered gent galloped off toward one of the corrals, his partner galloping after him and casting a skeptical glance back over his shoulder at Yakima.

"Don't mind them," came a girl's seemingly disembodied but familiar voice. "If you had to ride around all day in the hot sun trying to hold the wolves at bay, getting paid pennies and piss water, allowed to visit town only once a month to bleed off your sap, you'd have a knot in your tail, too."

Yakima swung around to see her standing on the other side of the wrought-iron gate, staring through the slender, black bars at him.

Emma smiled.

"Shit."

"Hi, Yakima." She smiled more broadly, showing her perfect white teeth, and gave a slow, flirtatious blink.

"I thought you'd be out keeping the raptors away from that gold-laden church."

"I'll probably ride out later and check on it." Emma slipped the gate's latching bolt, closed her hands around the angling bars, and pushed the gate open. It groaned on its hinges. The girl stepped out with the gate and wrapped her arms around Yakima's neck, rising up on her toes to kiss him.

He drew his head back, pushed her away.

"Knock it off."

"Spoilsport."

He stared down at her. It was almost as though he were looking at someone else—a completely different girl from the Emma Kosgrove he'd come to know. Gone were her dusty riding clothes and brown Stetson. Today she wore a conservatively styled, cream, gingham housedress printed with tiny yellow sunflowers. The frock was buttoned clear up to her throat and was trimmed with a narrow, lace-edged collar. The collar was closed with a gold cameo pin.

The dress was not meant to be sexy, but on this girl, how could it not be? The gingham was pulled taut across her high, firm breasts, and the cream color accented the

147

tan, earthy beauty of her face. Her hair, bleached the color of flax straw by her hours riding through these mountains in the harsh desert sun, was freshly washed and brushed. Sausage curls hung down against her cheeks. Several strands from each temple had been drawn back around behind her head and secured with a gold clip to tumble down her slender back.

His admiration must have been plain in his expression.

She broke the pout off, smiling, eyes flashing. "I clean up right well, wouldn't you say?" She shook the sausage curls back from her cheeks, threw her shoulders back, and thrust out her breasts. He tried not to remember cupping the bare, sweet orbs in his hands and sticking his nose between them, inhaling her natural aroma, like an intoxicating elixir.

"Is your father here?" he asked, changing the subject.

Emma snagged his left arm in both of her arms and led him through the gate and along a flagstone walk through the shady orchard in which desert songbirds piped. "Of course. He invited you out here, didn't he?"

Yakima pulled his arm free and said, "What's it about?"

"Who knows? Poppa doesn't tell me anything about his business. Maybe he just wants to meet the marshal of Apache Springs."

"I doubt that."

"Well, I reckon you'll know soon, then. Right this way,

Marshal Henry," Emma said, raising her voice as she led him onto a broad, deep patio flanked by two heavy oak, ornately scrolled doors propped open to the midday air.

The deeply shaded, low-slung house had an old, Spanish air about it—one of Old World refinement—though judging by the good shape it was in, it had been built recently. The walls, probably comprised of native adobe bricks, had been finished in stucco and coated with whitewash that reflected the desert sun. Clay *botillas* hung from strips of dyed hemp from the patio's cottonwood rafters, the evaporating water cooling the air scented with the sharp tang of lemons.

As Emma led Yakima through the open doors, the citrus aroma was replaced by that of *piñon* smoke, likely from previous fires that had held the desert evening chill at bay. There was also the fragrance of a good cigar. Voices emanated from the house's dusky recesses, and then one voice—deep and masculine—fairly roared with anger:

"Tell them if they want to strike, I'll do everything in my power to break it! I'll drive those ungrateful bastards to their knees! Every last one! They'll never work in this country again. They can go back to fucking the diseased *putas* in Mexico, where most of them hail from! They can try to find a *patron* down there who treats them half as good I always have!"

Another man spoke briefly in a dramatically lower

voice before the shouting man shouted once more, after slapping his hand hard on something solid—a desktop, perhaps: "They'll get paid in a couple of days—when Salko returns from the Southern Pacific tracks! Salko is transporting the payroll! Tell them if they strike now, they won't get paid a fucking dime!"

The man with the softer, less passionate voice spoke again, and then footsteps sounded. A door opened on the far side of the salon, or parlor, that Emma had led Yakima into. A slender man in a three-piece suit and handlebar mustache stepped through the door, walking quickly, setting a black bowler hat on his bald head.

He appeared to be in his early forties or so—a dapper gent with a skinny neck and prominent Adam's apple and, at the moment, a very flushed face with glassily anxious eyes. As he moved into the *salon* he slowed to a near stop, his gaze taking the measure of the big, badge-wearing half-breed standing beside Emma.

"Oh," the man said, continuing to walk past Yakima, as though he were reluctant to come to a full stop and risk more of the previous tirade. "Oh... you're... you're *him,* aren't you?"

The dapper gent raised his curious gaze to Yakima's face, no doubt studying the piercing jade eyes set deep in red sockets.

"The rock-worshippin' town marshal from Apache

Springs?" Yakima asked, dryly. "Yep."

"Ah, well... I see." The dapper gent dipped his chin to Emma and pinched the narrow brim of his crisp bowler in parting. "Miss Kosgrove."

"Luther," Emma said.

Luther retreated back through the house, using the same route Emma had led her guest along.

"Luther Hammersmith is the superintendent of the Conquistador," Emma told Yakima, keeping her voice low as though in deference to the obvious fiery emotion still emanating from the door Luther had left open behind him. "Poor bastard has his work cut out for him. He's the fourth one since Poppa brought me and Julia out from the east—nearly seven years ago now. They don't last long."

"Who's that?" came the same voice as that of the shouter, though he was no longer shouting but yelling. "Emma? Emma, is that you?" A silhouette appeared in the hall outside the open door through which Luther had fled. A short, stocky silhouette wreathed in gray cigar smoke.

"It's me, Poppa."

"What're you saying?"

"Nothing, Poppa." Emma canted a rebellious smirk up at Yakima.

"I heard you!"

"Oh, for chrissakes!" Emma retorted, her own eyes flashing furiously. "It's nothing that isn't true. I was just telling Yakima… er, Marshal Henry, who has arrived, by the way… how things fly out here at the Conquistador!"

"You know I don't like talking out of school, young lady!"

"Then you should keep your voice down, you long-winded old tyrant!" Again, Emma smirked up at Yakima, who was more than a little taken aback by the daughter-father exchange, as heated as it seemed.

Hugh Kosgrove walked out of the shadows of the short hall branching off from the *salon* and into the light angling in from the tall, deeply recessed windows lining both sides of the large, high-ceilinged room appointed in heavy Spanish furniture upholstered mostly in dark cowhide. Yakima was surprised by the man's appearance. He'd seen Kosgrove only in passing from afar, but somehow, he'd envisioned a much different sort than the man moving toward him now—a portly gent shaped like a rain barrel and standing well under six feet tall.

Despite his girth, Hugh Kosgrove moved quickly, taking short, mincing steps, swinging his hips and shoulders far to each side, throwing his arms back as though he were moving through water. He had short, curly, gray hair, bright-blue eyes teeming with ironic good humor, a small, plump nose that was a patchwork of broken and frayed blood vessels, and a ruddy face mottled red from the sun. Untrimmed muttonchops the same color as his hair trailed to his lower jaw.

He was smiling brightly, more than a little ironically, an expression his face seemed entirely comfortable with and accustomed to.

The mine owner appeared of English or Irish extraction and spoke in a thick eastern brogue, but he wore a Spanish-style white, silk shirt open halfway down his mottled, red chest, and Spanish-cut corduroy slacks tucked into the tops of polished, black, Spanish-style boots adorned with lavish red and white stitching. Yakima's immediate impression was of a boisterous easterner, possibly a former street fighter from an east-coast city, who'd made a fortune probably working both sides of the law and come west to amuse himself by trying on a new culture like a fresh suit of clothes—and digging for gold.

"How do you like how this high-blooded little filly talks to her old man, Marshal Henry? I guess it's fairly obvious I spared the rod on this one, eh?"

Yakima could see now that the heated verbiage Kosgrove and his comely daughter had exchanged had all been bluster, and that such forms of communication were the custom of the country out here. Probably had been since his two girls had moved out here to live with their old man after their mother, from whom Kosgrove had been divorced, had died back east.

"It's never too late," Yakima said, cutting his wry gaze

between father and daughter.

"Oh, it's far too late," Emma said, sidling up to Hugh Kosgrove and brushing her open hand over the tops of their heads, indicating that she was taller than her father by a good two or three inches.

"A big girl," Kosgrove said. "Just like her mother."

The sudden switch in tone to a biting sharpness was likely customary with old Kosgrove, as well. Yakima could tell the barb—probably an oft-used weapon—hit its mark. Emma flushed but, a veteran of such skirmishes, recovered quickly.

With aplomb, gesturing at her father with her open hand, she said, "Yakima Henry, Hugh Kosgrove, blustering son of a bitch and my father, as well as owner of the Conquistador. Hugh Kosgrove, also known as Poppa Bear"—she leaned down to plant a warm kiss on the old man's right cheek while glancing ironically up at Yakima—"this is Yakima Henry, marshal of Apache Springs in the Arizona Territory."

"Yeah, yeah," Kosgrove said, apparently growing irate at his daughter's overly patronizing tone. "I know what territory I'm in. And I know where Apache Springs is, as well. Lord knows I've put enough money into that town of late. Those bastards are strapping me for cash, say there's gonna be a big payoff after the railroad chugs into town. Well, we'll see, we'll see. Anyway..."

Kosgrove held out his thick, little hand, and Yakima shook it. "Pleased to meet you finally, Marshal Henry. I've always meant to thank you for what you did to get Julia back safely from that devil Rebel Wilkes." He frowned from Yakima to his daughter still standing beside him, Emma's arm draped across the old man's thick shoulders. "And managing to keep this one alive while doing it."

"Couldn't have done it without her... and my deputy."

"Pshaw!" Emma said with ironic self-deprecation, then changed the subject. "Three wolves told me several minutes ago that dinner is ready and waiting, gentlemen. It's probably cold by now. Shall we?"

The young woman swung around, skirts swirling, and strode through a broad arched doorway in the *salon*'s far wall. Kosgrove gestured with his hand, and Yakima followed the girl from the *salon* into a dining room boasting a long, solid wooden table surrounded by high-backed wooden chairs.

A slender man with the features of a full-blood Indian and dressed in a white silk jacket and string tie was just then setting a silver coffee pot in the middle of the table. Already on the table were the victuals of the noon dinner—a large turkey roasted to a golden brown and stuffed with oyster dressing, a bowl heaping with snowy mashed potatoes, a steaming china boat chockfull of rich brown milk gravy, a bowl of creamed corn, and another of the greenest green beans Yakima had ever laid eyes on—obviously picked and cooked fresh from a nearby, irrigated garden.

There were two straw-basketed demijohns of dark-red wine. Crystal wine glasses glistened before three large platters set upon the table's far left end—one at the very end and two at the corners, one across from the other. The silverware shone with almost painful brightness in a shaft of golden sunlight angling through a long window to the right.

"Marshal Henry," Emma said, indicating the plate on the table's near side. "Father will take his throne at his customary place at the end there."

She swung around and placed her hands atop the shoulders of the Indian just then filling her wine glass across the table from where Yakima was now standing. "This is Three Moons, our, uh, butler, for lack of a better word."

She glanced at the slender Indian, roughly her own height, who had long, almond shaped eyes and a broad, round face with a beak-like Apache nose hooking down over his thick, slightly upturned upper lip. The abundant silver streaks in his hair said that he was maybe Kosgrove's age, which Yakima assumed to be late fifties to early sixties. Still, the Indian was board straight, and there were few lines in his handsome, aboriginal face with its coal-black eyes set beneath thin, gray-black brows and a high forehead back from which his raven-black hair had been pulled. It trailed down his back in twin braids.

"Three Moons, this is Yakima Henry, town marshal of Apache Springs," Emma said, glancing with a little more charm and faintly jeering humor than Yakima would have liked.

"Pleased to meet you, Three Moons."

"The pleasure is all mine, Mister Henry," the Indian said, shoving a cork into the mouth of the wine bottle. He owned not a trace of the customary clipped-vowel and rolled-consonant accent of the usual Native American. He spoke like a white man—a well-bred and -educated one, at that. "Congratulations on the position. I expect it keeps you hopping?"

"It does at that," Yakima returned.

"Yakima was the lawman in Apache Springs when that bunch burned and looted the town a couple of years back," Hugh Kosgrove told his servant, who stood as though at attention, hands folded before him, chin up, near the far corner of the table. "He ran them down, killed every one, brought the loot and my oldest daughter back safely."

"So I heard," Three Moons said, dipping his chin respectfully.

"I had a little help from the Rio Grande Kid and

someone else." Yakima crooked a smile across the table at Emma, who'd taken her seat.

Emma smiled with a little too much double meaning at him and shook out her napkin. Yakima glanced at Kosgrove. The old mine owner didn't seem to suspect just what exactly his dinner guest and his comely daughter had meant to each other out in the high-and-rocky of the Sierra Estrada.

But then Yakima turned his glance to the Indian servant, Three Moons, who quirked a crooked smile. Kosgrove might not have known, but his Indian servant sure as hell did.

Yakima's ears warmed.

"Three Moons and I," Kosgrove said, standing behind his chair, resting his hands on its back, his cigar smoldering between the first and second fingers of his right one, "we been through a lot together over the years. I met him back east, though he grew up here in Arizona. He was educated in Boston after bein' taken in by missionaries with money. We came west together nigh on twenty years ago now. He knew the Apaches—or, at least he knew the Chiricahuas—well enough to keep us both from getting slow cooked over a low fire. And, by hook and by crook, I learned about rocks from books—after I taught myself to read, that is—while fighting the Germans and Italians in the old neighborhood. And so"—Kosgrove smiled admiringly at his Indian companion—"here we are now. Two old men sipping bourbon at night by the fire, remembering the wild old days."

Emma turned to Three Moons and rattled off several sentences in what Yakima recognized as the language spoken by the Chiricahua Apache.

Three Moons looked down and snorted a laugh.

"What?" Kosgrove said, scowling at his daughter. "What'd she say? Consarn it, Emma—haven't I told you it ain't polite for you two to speak that in front of me when you know I don't know a lick of it!"

"She said the old coyote is getting sentimental in his old age," Yakima said.

All eyes turned to him, arched in surprise.

The half-breed shrugged. "I was a scout at Fort Hildebrandt not all that long ago," he explained. "Heart of Chiricahua country."

"Fort Hell." Three Moons nodded in acknowledgement. "Appropriately named. Or so I hear. God didn't dwell there."

"He means it true—about God," Kosgrove told Yakima. "Three Moons is an ordained Lutheran minister, though you wouldn't know it by lookin' at him."

"And you wouldn't know that by looking at you, you old whore monger," Three Moons said in Chiricahua, grinning between Emma and Yakima, "that his mother was a horny old coyote and his father was a three-legged armadillo!"

Emma and Three Moons threw their heads back, laughing.

Yakima chuckled.

"You cussed Injun!" Kosgrove railed in mock fury. "I think I smell your dog stew burning out in the kitchen!"

13

Yakima couldn't remember when he'd last enjoyed a mid-day meal as much as he enjoyed dinner at the Kosgrove house. Three Moons was one hell of a cook. Yakima had no complaints. At least, not about the food.

While Hugh Kosgrove rambled on about rocks and geology and Mexican liquor—his favorite being *bacanora*—as well as about his frequent trips deeper into the mountains looking for another gold-rich vein, Emma kept casting lusty looks across the table at her and her father's guest. She obviously took great pleasure in making Yakima remember their nights together under the desert stars, making him squirm now in his chair in her father's elegant, Spanish-style *casa*.

At the same time, remembering those nights against his will, he couldn't help feeling a hot pull of lust deep in his nether regions, which made him keep his eyes on his plate as he forked the succulent food into his mouth, nodding automatically, chuckling occasionally at the long-winded Kosgrove's tales of his gold-hunting exploits.

Despite these distractions, a vague curiosity catfooted around inside his brain.

Why was he here?

He knew he hadn't been summoned merely to enjoy Three Moons's cooking or to become acquainted with Hugh Kosgrove. Those were merely the gold braid on the envelope of his invitation. The old gold miner had called Yakima out here for a different reason, and, as Three Moons cleared the dishes of the main meal and then served peach cobbler and coffee, it became clear Kosgrove was waiting till later to broach the purpose of Yakima's visit—likely when he and his guest were alone.

Sure enough, as soon as dessert was over, Kosgrove licked his fork clean, like a dog polishing off a particularly sweet bone, tossed it onto his empty plate, belched, farted, leaned back in his chair, and turned to Yakima. "Marshal Henry, why don't we repair to my office? I have a particular matter I'd like to discuss with you."

He glanced at Emma with a patronizing smile and patted her hand atop the table. "Boring business talk, child. Why don't you help Three Moons with the dishes?"

Emma rolled her eyes.

When Yakima had taken a seat in a leather-upholstered

guest chair fronting Kosgrove's large desk in an office easily the size of a suite in a fancy big-city hotel, Kosgrove offered him a cigar from a cedar humidor.

Yakima declined. His curiosity was piqued. He wanted the man to get on with business. Or whatever the hell it was he'd lured Yakima out here to discuss.

Taking a cigar for himself, Kosgrove removed the tip with a silver clip, then strolled over to a long, open glass door looking out onto the *casa's* shaded patio, where a large, tiger-striped cat lay sunning itself near a birdbath. Between the cat's paws lay the remains of a dead yellow-headed blackbird—a few tufts of down and yellow feathers, part of a black wing.

A cabinet clock ticked woodenly against the wall behind Yakima, metronomic beats that, in his languor following the heavy meal, threatened to make him sleepy.

When Kosgrove had got his stogie going, he blew a long plume out onto the patio and said, "I want you to stop seeing her."

The order, given so casually, was puzzling at first. Then, when he'd understood the words, Yakima thought: Oh, shit—he knows about Emma and me. His heart thudded, remembering those intoxicating, erotic nights at his old stone cabin in the Javelina Bluffs, in which he'd holed up after first coming to the Sierra Estrada. Damn her. Her brash glances across the table had given them away.

163

Kosgrove turned to Yakima, one brow arched, a bitter smile on his thin-lipped mouth. "You think I didn't know?"

Yakima winced with embarrassment. "Look, Mister Kosgrove, I—"

"Of course, it got back to me. Everyone in town knows."

"In town?" Yakima rarely, if ever, saw Emma in town.

"You're making me a laughing stock."

"I... I don't understand."

"I can't ride into the Springs for a business meeting without hearing the whispering behind my back, see the townsfolk snickering." Kosgrove's ruddy face grew gradually red with anger as he took a few puffs from his cigar and said, "My oldest daughter nearly marries Rebel Wilkes—the man who double-crosses me by staking out his own mining claim on *my time,* when he *should have been working for me!*—and then burns and murders half the town. That wasn't enough for her, though, was it? *Then* she marries an even lesser sort—Lon Taggart—the marshal of Apache Springs. A workaday man from a bad family who was going no farther than that badge!"

He pointed at the five-starred chunk of silver-chased tin pinned to Yakima's buckskin tunic.

Kosgrove took another few puffs off the stogie, his face red and swollen now, blue eyes bright with rage. "Then, when Taggart swallows a pill he can't digest, she takes into her bed the next marshal of Apache Springs—*a half-breed Indian*!"

It was all clear to Yakima now. Kosgrove didn't mean Emma.

He meant Julia.

Yakima rose slowly, choking back the fury rising inside him. He glared at the older man facing him from the open doorway, wreathed in a thick, gray cloud of aromatic cigar smoke.

Calm, he told himself. Calm. This isn't a saloon, and you're not drunk on firewater. No tearing the place apart!

He had to repeat the silent admonition several times.

"She told me she loves me. I love her."

Kosgrove laughed without mirth and narrowed his blue eyes caustically. "Come on! What could come of it? *Marriage?*"

Yakima didn't respond. He just stood glowering at the man sneering at him.

"Children?" Kosgrove added with the same derision.

Still, Yakima glowered at him, fighting the rage building and building inside him, his ears ringing like a boiling teapot.

"What would such children look like? How would they be treated in Apache Springs? If you love her, imagine how she would be treated in Apache Springs, or anywhere else, for that matter!"

"That's a decision for her to make."

"My daughter, Marshal Henry... well, you probably know by now. Julia is not always the most sensible in these matters. For God sakes, she almost married the man who double-crossed me, then burned the town when the town boosters wouldn't let him run a train through town to his proposed mine!" Kosgrove laughed as though it had all been an insane joke. "And then she marries Taggart against my wishes, against my threats to cut her out of my life as well as my will!"

Yakima didn't point out that Kosgrove himself had arranged for Julia to marry Rebel Wilkes, Kosgrove's mining engineer, as part of an informal business deal. It would have been a waste of time. Kosgrove had revised his point of view on the topic, and, having dealt with such arrogant, self-centered men before—many of them, in fact—Yakima knew there was no changing it. The man had made up his mind that his oldest daughter had been born to defy him out of spite, and he'd go to his grave with that opinion, however wrong.

Yakima knew—at least *sensed*—that Julia actually loved her father and, deep down, wanted nothing more than to please him. That's why she'd agreed to marry Wilkes. After that had soured, with no little relief to Julia, who'd never loved Wilkes in the first place, she'd realized that pleasing her father was an impossible feat. Having nearly driven herself mad with trying, and knowing the lengths Kosgrove would go to to make her toe his line, she'd gone to the other extreme.

Not that she hadn't loved Taggart. She had. Not that she didn't love Yakima. He knew she did. But a part of what had first attracted her to both Taggart and Yakima was knowing that her father wouldn't approve. Yakima didn't hold it against her in the least. It was the result of her strained relationship with her father and an ironic fact of her life.

Yakima walked slowly across the office to stand before Kosgrove. He consciously relaxed his muscles. He didn't want to seem any more threatening than his size already made him appear. This was not an occasion for violence. Sober, he was above all that. Especially now that he wore the badge.

"Mister Kosgrove, I know you're—"

"Even Three Moons agrees!" Kosgrove continued, staring up at Yakima through his smoke cloud. "Ask him yourself if you think this is only about you. It's not. Three Moons married a white woman back east. You know what happened? The girl's father took a gun into his attic and shot himself out of shame! Shame despite that Three Moons had gone to none other than Harvard University and earned a degree in divinity! Now, I'm not saying I'd shoot myself," Kosgrove added, laughing loudly, caustically. "No, no. Not me. I relay the story merely to illustrate the scandal such a union can cause. Especially in these parts, with so many folks so recently terrorized by the Apaches. Not that you're Apache, but—"

"Kosgrove, shut up and listen to me."

The old man glowered up at him, his blue eyes flashing as though from a fire burning inside his head.

"I know you love your daughter and you think you know what's best for her. But you don't." Yakima set his hat on his head and started walking toward the door.

"One thousand dollars."

Yakima stopped at the door and turned back to the old man now taking another couple of draws off his cigar and grinning shrewdly. Yakima laughed. He grabbed the doorknob and started to turn it but stopped when Kosgrove said, "I do apologize, but you're forcing my hand here, Marshal Henry."

Yakima drew the door open but glanced over his shoulder at Kosgrove again, vaguely curious. The man had pitched his voice with an ominous edge.

"I really didn't think it would come to this." Kosgrove walked toward his desk. "Close the door."

Yakima sighed and closed the door only because he was curious about what the man was going to pluck out of his basket next. However, a cool breath of apprehension blew against his ears.

Kosgrove walked around behind the desk and pulled open the middle drawer. He withdrew a swollen manila envelope and tossed it to the opposite side of his desk.

"A thousand dollars, and this conversation goes no further. A thousand dollars to stay away from my daughter. I'm not ordering you to leave town. By all accounts, you're a good lawman. We need a good lawman in Apache Springs."

"I gave you my answer." Yakima turned to the door again.

"I'm sorry to have to do this."

Once again, Yakima turned back to Kosgrove. He half expected the man to pull a gun out of the same drawer. It wasn't a gun he produced, however. It was a quarter-folded sheet of paper. He tossed it over by the money.

Yakima walked to the desk and stared down at the folded, slightly yellowed cream leaf.

Again, that cool breath of apprehension blew against his ears. It was as though he were staring down at a dagger with his own blood on it.

Slowly, haltingly, he picked up the paper and unfolded it.

A cold stone dropped in his belly when he saw the word *WANTED* splashed across the top of the paper in large, heavy black letters. Below, in a box taking up roughly a third of the sheet, was a penciled likeness, or a

169

rough likeness, of himself, complete with long hair and low-crowned, flat-brimmed hat. Between *WANTED* and the penciled picture was a block of regular-sized type in capital letters:

$2500 REWARD FOR INFORMATION LEADING TO CAPTURE OF UNKNOWN KILLER OF DEPUTY US MARSHAL LEON MYERS IN BURLINSON HOTEL, ESTELLE, KANSAS, ON NIGHT OF JUNE 6. GREEN-EYED HALF-BREED. NAME UNKNOWN. LEFT TOWN NEXT MORNING ON A BLAZE-FACED BLACK STALLION.

Yakima hadn't realized he'd been holding his breath. Now, slowly, he released it as he just as slowly set the Wanted circular back down on the edge of Kosgrove's desk.

"Mighty bad business—killing a deputy United States marshal," the gold miner said. He was leaning forward, fists on his desk.

He stared with menace across the desk at Yakima. "They didn't have a name, and it's not a very good likeness. That's probably why no one has run you down. Yet. My good friend, Lloyd Barstow, who runs the Western Union and Wells Fargo office in Apache Springs, was cleaning out a drawer in his office when he found this near the bottom. He decided to turn it over to me. Asked me what I thought should be done about it."

"And you said…"

"Nothing. As long as there's no need." Kosgrove shrugged his heavy shoulders. "Kansas is a long ways away. This happened three years ago. And… I'm thinking maybe this Myers fella, federal lawman or not, needed killing."

"He did."

"I'll take your word for that…"

"As long as I stop seeing Julia." Yakima heard the emotional quaver in his voice.

Kosgrove's only response to that was a slow blink as he lifted his cigar to his mouth once more and let several more puffs blossom around his face set with a subtly victorious smile. Yakima stared at him, that ringing in his ears now rising to the din of cracked bells echoing from a near tower. His urge was to swing his arm across the desk, to smash his fist into Kosgrove's smugly smiling face.

If he'd had a few belts in him, he'd have done just that. But he was as sober as a judge, so he didn't have the firewater for an excuse. Still, he felt as though he were about to explode. Instead of waiting around to find out what he'd do, given enough time and rage, he willed himself away from the desk, stumbling a little on his spurs, the rowels raking the flagstone tiles.

The room was a little blurry, and the floor was rising and falling around him. He didn't feel drunk so much as drugged, or as though he'd been thrown on his head.

He turned toward the door. He had to reach for the knob twice before he finally grabbed it, opened the door, and stumbled out into the hall. He steadied himself against a wall, then strode back through the house, hearing Emma call his name distantly from somewhere behind him.

Then he was outside, crossing the front patio, pushing through the wrought-iron gate with the *KOSGROVE* name scrolled in its center, striding quickly across the yard toward where his horse waited in the corral, staring over the gate at him, as though Wolf had sensed the trouble inside the house and was expecting his rider to come for him.

Julia.

Yakima slung his saddle onto the black's back, slipped the bridle over its ears. He kicked open the gate and galloped out of the corral, out of the yard.

A mile, maybe two—hell, maybe three—slid by in a blur of blind emotion.

What snapped him out of it, albeit briefly, was a searing pain in his left arm and the following crack of a rifle from somewhere in the bluffs above the trail he was following.

Wolf whinnied and lurched up off his front hooves, scissoring his front legs furiously at the sky.

Another bullet plumed dust near the stallion's prancing hooves. Yakima had let the reins slip out of his hands when the first bullet had punched into his arm. He reached for them now, but then the reins and Wolf were gone. There was nothing around him but air. The gray-brown slant of a steep slope rose up quickly to smack him hard about the head and shoulders.

He cried out in shock and agony.

And then he was rolling... rolling... rolling down an endless and endlessly brutal, rocky slope.

14

Yakima lifted his head, groaned.

He opened his eyes. The world was a tan blur around him, the sun slashing at his corneas.

He closed his eyes, rested his head back against the gravelly ground. He felt as though he'd been run over by a runaway ore dray. His back and neck felt broken. His shoulders and arms, too. Legs and hips—same thing. Multiple bruises probably made by the rocks and gravel and sandstone lumps he'd rolled over when falling from the steep slope converged to make his entire body feel like one massive, generalized, purple, fast-swelling slab of misery.

Gradually, he became aware of a slightly different ache in his left arm. It was a sharp, searing pain. He turned and dipped his chin, saw the blood stain around the tear in his tunic sleeve, about seven inches down from his shoulder. He also saw the blood dribbling onto the rocks and red sand and gravel beneath that arm.

He remembered the bullet. Alarm rose past the physical agony hammering his bones and muscles. Quickly, he took stock of his condition, tensing and then slackening various parts of his body, moving his arms and legs, turning his head. Despite the pain he was in, he didn't think anything was broken. Now that he had that decided as best as he could at the moment, before he'd done any real moving around, he considered his situation.

He'd been shot out of his saddle. From the left side of the trail. He wasn't sure how long ago that had been. In his addled state, he wasn't sure how long he'd been lying here, unconscious. Or maybe he'd *just* landed here.

As his body was a mass of agony, his mind was fuzzy with confusion. Judging by the sun's angle, he hadn't been here all that long. Whoever had shot him was likely somewhere atop the ridge he'd fallen from, possibly still looking to finish the job they'd started.

Still lying flat, chest expanding and contracting quickly as he breathed, tension rising in him, Yakima looked down toward his right thigh. He knew a moment's relief to see that his stag-butted .44 was still in its holster. He dropped his hand over the revolver, used his index finger to free the keeper thong from over the hammer.

He tensed with a start when a voice, ominously clear in

the dry desert air, said with menacing matter-of-factness, "Go ahead and put another bullet in him, Les."

The man who must have been Les said, "Why don't you do it?"

"You got the better angle."

"Yeah, but the footing here is for shit."

"Just take the goddamn shot! Finish off the bastard!"

Yakima lifted his head and squinted up the long, steep slope before him and down which he'd tumbled. It took a while for his vision to clear.

Then he saw them—two men on the slope about fifty yards above him, spread out about thirty feet apart. There was a thumb of ground just above Yakima, giving him partial cover from one of the two rifle-wielding bushwhackers. The other man was moving daintily along a talus slide, crouched low and carefully setting his boots, heading toward a boulder humping out of the slope just below him.

Yakima grunted as he slid the .44 from its holster. He wished like hell he had his Yellowboy, but the rifle was still in its scabbard on Wolf's back, wherever Wolf was…

Yakima grunted again as he clicked the hammer back, narrowed one eye, and aimed down the barrel of the pistol. He drew a bead on the bushwhacker just then dropping to a knee atop the boulder, raising his rifle. Yakima nudged the barrel of the .44 a little higher, adjusting for the distance as well as the steepness of the slope. It was a long shot for a handgun.

Yakima held his breath, squeezed the trigger.

The .44 bucked and roared.

The bullet plumed rock dust off the edge of the boulder near the bushwhacker's boots. The man jerked back with a start, yelling, "Shit!" He dropped to his butt.

The other man laughed jeeringly.

As the shooter rose again, getting his boots beneath him, Yakima's Colt barked again, smoke and flames jetting up the slope. The man on the boulder jerked once more, even more violently this time.

For a second, he crouched there on one knee, staring down the slope toward Yakima. Slowly, his Winchester wilted in his right hand.

"Les?" the other man said.

Les lowered his head and fell slowly forward. Dropping the rifle, he tumbled over the edge of the boulder. He hit the slope on his back, his black hat tumbling away, his black chaps flapping like wings as he rolled. Twenty feet from where Yakima had dropped him, the man bounced off a boulder with a dull smack and veered down the slope nearly straight above where the half-breed lay, crowding the base of the slope to stay out of view of the second bushwhacker.

Les rolled and rolled, arms and legs flying, dust billowing around him. Longish, red-blond hair danced around his head. He grew larger and larger before Yakima until the half-breed pulled his head back, and Les flew straight over him to land on the canyon floor just beyond him.

Yakima turned to his left, staring out across his own wounded left arm.

Les lay ten feet away on his back. His head was turned toward Yakima. He had coarse, straight, blond hair and a blond mustache. His chaps were black. *Chaperreras* was what the Mexican whore, Clara, had called them in her native tongue. This was the man who'd visited her room to talk about an upcoming job with the blue-eyed man. "Eyes with no good in them," Clara had called them.

Yakima looked at Les's face. The man's eyes were open and staring at Yakima. Blood trickled out both sides of the man's mouth to dribble down over his chin. The hole in his upper right chest oozed blood down the front of his blue and red checked shirt. His chest rose and fell slowly.

He stared at Yakima, but it was impossible to tell if he was seeing anything. His chest was still moving, so there was still some life in him.

Keeping his head below the hump of sand and gravel, Yakima said, "Les, what job you boys got planned?"

Les moved his lips a little. He moved them again until finally a choked whisper escaped them. "Fuck you, you dog-eatin' Injun. You... you killed me... you *fucker*!"

Les Reese made a strangling sound, and his eyes brightened in horror until they grew opaque, and his chest fell still.

Yakima turned and edged a cautious glance up over the hump of ground covering him from the other man—the man with the dead blue eyes? Apprehension swirled in his belly when he saw the man was no longer standing where he'd been standing before, about halfway up the slope and between two talus slides.

Yakima looked around, his heart thudding.

No sign of the man. After carefully perusing the slope above and to both sides and seeing nothing moving, not even a cloud shadow, he tossed a look along the canyon in which he'd fallen. A jumble of large boulders lay to the south. They littered the slope to that side of the chasm. That must be where the second bushwhacker had gone, maybe trying to work his way into a better position to send a killing shot into his prey.

Straight back behind Yakima stood a narrow corridor between two jagged walls of broken rock. The corridor apparently led deeper into the canyon. It was Yakima's only way out. Or at least his only way from where he lay now, certain prey to the second son of a bitch with a rifle.

A light breeze rose, lifting sand and other debris and swirling it around the canyon. Somewhere in the brassy sky above, a *zopilate* gave its chilling carrion cry.

Yakima pressed a hand against the ground, heaved himself to a squatting position, looking around quickly, feeling the crawling sensation of having rifle sights being planted between his shoulder blades. He still wasn't sure he could move as well as he needed to—his body cried out in misery as he continued to straighten—but he had no choice but to lurch forward and move as quickly as possible toward the gap in the wall of fallen boulders.

Something shredded the air just behind him.

The bullet hammered the ridge to his left, three feet back.

Yakima cursed, grinding his molars against the pain burning through him, and quickened his pace, lunging into a shambling run. Two more shots screeched behind him, spanging shrilly off rocks. Then Yakima was in the corridor, jogging along a high-sided arroyo, following its twists and curves.

When the wall on his right lowered, something moved beyond it.

Yakima jerked his head in that direction, saw a man standing on the steep slope on that side of the narrow canyon—a pot-bellied, dark-haired, dark-mustached man wearing a dirty, sweaty, pinstriped shirt and suspenders. Fringed, brown leather chaps buffeted about his denim-clad legs.

He snapped a Henry rifle to his shoulder. Yakima

threw himself forward, dropping to his knees behind a four-foot-high snag of brush and rock.

A bullet sliced through the air where his head had been and slammed into the slope to his left.

The bushwhacker's rifle cracked, echoing.

Yakima winced as he again lurched to his feet, swung his right arm up, hastily aimed his .44, and sent two quick shots toward that side of the canyon. Both bullets tore up gouts of rock and sand where his stalker had been standing before he'd thrown himself with a curse behind the cover of a small boulder.

Yakima continued running, boulders and rock snags now shielding him from the canyon's far side.

He followed the canyon's course around to the left.

His pursuer shouted, "You're a dead man, breed!"

Two quick rifle shots, the bullets sailing high over Yakima's head.

He kept jogging, glancing up and to his right, occasionally swinging around to look behind him. Silence fell over the canyon, interrupted occasionally by the breeze snagging on the high cliff walls to each side, rustling the brush of the old flood snags choking the canyon floor, creating natural bottlenecks.

He was following a meandering game path now, breathless, his arm feeling as though a razor-edged, hot blade were sawing into the wound. He was losing too much blood. He needed water. He needed to clean the wound and bind it.

But at the moment, all he could do was run. He had only his .44, and his stalker had a Henry repeater. The bastard also had the advantage of not having a bullet in him.

Yakima ran under a natural stone arch. Beyond the arch, the arroyo dropped severely to the right. Yakima followed it down to where the air was cool but also fouled by the smell of something dead and rotting in the sun. The gravel was damp beneath his boots. Water dribbled from a crenellated wall of rock crusted with minerals and dark-green moss.

Yakima crouched to slurp water from two thin streams, licking the cold substance into his mouth and swallowing. The water braced him. He needed more, his thirst awakening now at the taste of it. He heard the faint, quick jingle of spurs behind him.

The second son of a bitch was dogging him. Maybe fifty, sixty yards back, but closing fast.

Yakima brushed cool water across his face, then continued running, following the old streambed's twisting course between canyon walls of various heights. When the canyon floor dropped again, abruptly and steeply, the air smelling of damp rock and mushrooms, he had the uneasy sensation that the earth was swallowing him.

Still, he ran. Jogged, rather.

He chewed his cheek against the ache in every bone and muscle, against the raw, hammering pain in his left arm, that sleeve now soaked with dark-red blood.

He wasn't sure how much farther he'd run before his legs gave out under him. It was as though he'd been tripped. He dropped to his knees and rolled. He rolled onto his back and, still clenching the Colt in his right hand, lay breathing as desperately as a landed fish, staring at the sky. His vision had darkened, and he didn't think it was only because clouds had now slid over the canyon.

He was on the verge of passing out.

By force of will, he sat up and looked around. Ahead, choking off the floor of the canyon was a broad pile of boulders that had likely tumbled down the rocky ridges. He cursed as he heaved himself to his feet, lumbered forward, and threw himself over the first, slanted boulder. He crawled over it and onto the next one, glancing into the dark gaps around him, dreading the appearance of a rattlesnake or a scorpion, possibly a Gila monster calling such a cavern home.

Something peeped in one of the gaps but it sounded like a packrat. A gecko slithered up and over a rock nearby, expanding its tiny green cheeks.

Grunting and sighing and muttering oaths under his breath, Yakima continued climbing until he'd crested the jumbled pile. He slipped over the crest and dropped five feet nearly straight down to the next boulder below, landing on his hip and shoulder with a loud, anguished groan.

Damn, that was a hard landing...

He choked off another groan and pricked his ears, listening, wondering if the groan had been picked up by his stalker.

He held very still, staring up at the crest of the boulder snag five feet above him, holding the Colt barrel up in his right hand, thumb on the hammer. He breathed through his mouth, chest rising and falling sharply. Sweat bathed him, streaming down his cheeks and into his shirt. The tunic was pasted against his chest and back, but the air was so dry, he could feel it evaporating even as it oozed from his pores.

Faintly, he heard movement above him.

The sounds continued to grow—the soft scrapes and dull thuds of boot leather on rock. The man was moving up on him.

Yakima drew a deep breath, then consciously slowed his breathing. He could run no farther. He'd make his stand here.

Tensely, he stared up the crest of boulders above him.

A minute passed. Then another.

Then the rake of a boot on rock touched his ears.

Pebbles and red dirt dribbled down from a flat-topped boulder above and to his right. A shadow angled out across the boulders beside Yakima—stretching long in the dull, gray light. The shadow was capped by a broad-brimmed, high-crowned hat.

Yakima's heart quickened. His trigger finger tingled.

He ran his tongue across dry lips.

The man above him stepped into view. The man looked around, then dropped his chin, and Yakima saw the black mustache and cobalt-blue eyes set beneath the brim of a tan Stetson. Quickly, Yakima aimed the Colt. His arm and hand were weak, his aim uncertain. The man's eyes snapped wide in sudden fear, and he jerked his head back a half a wink before the Colt roared, stabbing flames and smoke straight up toward the crest of the boulder pile.

A miss—shit!

Yakima triggered the Colt again.

Ping!

In all the commotion, he hadn't remembered to fill the chamber he usually kept empty beneath the revolver's hammer. The wheel was empty.

15

Somewhere above Yakima, the man laughed.

The blue-eyed son of a bitch stepped back into view, raising his iron-framed Henry rifle to his shoulder and squinting one cobalt eye as he aimed down the octagonal barrel at Yakima's head. The man's body trembled, dropped a couple of inches. At the same time, the Henry thundered.

The bullet ricocheted off the rock Yakima knelt on, a foot to his left, causing the half-breed to flinch and jerk backward. When he looked up again, he saw that a rock that his assailant was standing on was tearing loose from a small chunk of sandy ground it had been embedded in.

"Oh, shit!" the man cried, crouching and throwing both arms out as though to balance himself.

The rock tore free, and the bushwhacker fell straight down at Yakima, who jerked back once more and twisted around, putting his back to the wall of boulders. The man and several rocks and a good bit of dirt and gravel dropped onto the boulder where Yakima had been a second before, and the blue-eyed bastard went flying several feet forward before rolling up against another, larger boulder.

Dust sifted through the air, obscuring Yakima's view.

The man sat up, hatless, grunting and groaning, shaking his head. His thick, black hair hung in his eyes. He shook it away, looked at Yakima, jerked with a start, and clawed at the six-shooter residing in a holster positioned for a cross-draw on his left hip.

Automatically, the half-breed's hand flung up behind his neck, sliding his Arkansas toothpick free of the hard leather sheath he wore under his shirt, behind his neck, strapped to a short, stiff leather lanyard.

He was so practiced in throwing the toothpick that he not so much aimed as merely watched the stiletto-like knife—five inches of Damascus steel tapering to a needle-like point—leave his hand to smoothly cleave the air, quickly closing the gap between him and the bushwhacker now aiming a long-barreled Smith & Wesson.

The knife plunged into the man's chest, just right of center.

He made a hiccupping sound as the Smithy bucked and roared, the bullet sailing skyward as the bushwhacker fell back against the boulder behind him. He dropped the pistol and looked down at the round, smooth, wooden handle of the toothpick bristling from his chest. Blood oozed up around the blade embedded nearly to its brass hilt.

As the dust cleared, the son of a bitch looked up at Yakima. His cobalt eyes appeared bleary, the light quickly fading in them. He leaned against the rock behind him, turned his head to one side, dropped his chin to his shoulder, gave a shudder, as though deeply chilled, and just sat there, his legs straight out before him.

He was as dead as his eyes had always been.

The thudding of horse hooves sounded, quickly growing louder.

Yakima jerked his knife from the dead man's chest, cleaned it on the man's shirt, and returned it to its scabbard. He picked up his Colt and quickly began reloading, his hands feeling as though he were wearing several pairs of bulky gloves. The light in him was diminishing fast. But he didn't have time to pass out. At least one more rider was heading toward him.

He'd just fumbled a third cartridge into the Colt's wheel when he saw a horse gallop out of the mouth of an off-shooting canyon. A blaze-faced black. Yakima squinted, studying the beast that stopped at the base of the boulder pile, near the mouth of the off-shooting canyon. As its dust caught up to it, the stallion shook its head and whinnied.

"Well, I'll… I'll be goddamned," Yakima raked out, chuckling despite his weariness. "Wolf, you son of a bitch, I… I thought you'd headed back to… to t-town." He smiled, pleased indeed. He finished reloading the Colt, filling every chamber, then flicking the loading gate closed and spinning the wheel.

"Hang on," he told the horse. "Be down in… three jangles of a… of a whore's bell…"

He heaved himself heavily to his feet. It took him a minute to get his balance. He was as weary and sore as he'd ever been, and he still leaked blood. Maybe not as much as before—the wound appeared to be clotting—but it was still running down his arm.

Thunder growled like a giant, angry dog in the sky.

Yakima looked up. The clouds were settling lower. He thought he felt a few small raindrops blowing against him on a fresh wind. The wind felt good. It blew his sweaty hair behind his head, dried the buckskin tunic pasted to his chest and shoulders.

He made his slow, cautious way over the rocks, choosing his steps carefully, avoiding possible snakes and cactus clumps. When he reached the canyon floor, Wolf trotted over to him and blew a greeting.

"How'd you find me?" Yakima slurred his words as

though drunk.

The horse whickered, sniffed his rider's bloody shoulder, and shook his head again.

"Just a nip," Yakima said, walking around to the horse's side to reset and tighten the saddle—not an easy task in his light-headed, badly fatigued condition.

When he'd managed to reset the saddle and tighten the latigo, the rain began to fall harder, splattering on the rocks around him and on the red *caliche* paving the canyon floor. Yakima had just turned out a stirrup and was about to poke his left boot through it, when lightning flashed on the canyon's far ridge—a piercing blue-red light.

Yakima lowered his foot and peered up at the rim.

A sprawling cedar was limned in a bright, electric blue, smoldering. Red flames and sparks burst from where the lightning had struck the tree, which now jackknifed forward over the canyon edge, cut in half. An earth-shuddering thunderclap followed the strike that left the tree a dancing ball of red flames.

The top half of the tree, cut away from the rest, plunged down onto the slope about fifty feet below the rim. It struck with a great crunching sound, exploding, and then its several burning and smoking pieces continued to roll down over the rocks strewn across the slope's shoulder.

Sidling close against Wolf, Yakima clung to his saddlehorn like a drunk to an awning support post as he peered up the ridge in amazement. "Shittt! You see that?"

Another rumbling sounded. At first, Yakima thought it was more thunder.

But then he could feel the ground quavering beneath his boots. He felt it shuddering through the stallion's body pressed up hard against his own. He looked up at the ridge again. It seemed to be moving—shaking.

His gut flip-flopped when two rocks dropped off the lip of the ridge. They were followed by another one, and then two more and then even more, and they were rolling down the ridge, crashing into others and causing those to break loose from their own moorings and roll, too.

They were maybe two hundred yards from where Yakima stood but heading toward him fast!

"This day isn't turning out so well," he said, trying to stick his left boot through his stirrup.

Wolf was skitter-hopping, nervous about the growing thunder of the boulders heading down the canyon wall. Yakima hopped on his right foot, cursing.

"Hold still, damn it, you broomtail cayuse!"

His right foot struck a stone sideways, and Yakima went down with a loud curse.

Hooves thundered. At first, he thought Wolf was galloping away from him again, but then he saw another horse and another rider gallop toward him from the off-shooting canyon, long hair the color of flax stems blowing back in the wind, beneath a brown Stetson.

"Yakima!" Emma cried.

The girl leaped from the saddle of her rangy buckskin. She glanced at the boulders rolling toward the canyon floor and crouched beside the half-breed, who was huffing and puffing like an old man as he tried hoisting himself back to his uncertain feet. His knees felt like putty, and he wasn't making it.

"You've been shot!" Emma cried as she grabbed his wounded arm and draped it around her neck, heaving them both to their feet.

"Ah, Christ, woman!" he yowled as the agony of her manhandling of his arm ripped through him.

"Don't be such a crybaby, and get into your saddle, you idiot!" She'd grabbed the prancing Wolf's reins and quickly led the horse over to where Yakima crouched, squeezing his wounded arm in his right hand. "Hurry!"

Emma held Wolf as steady as possible while Yakima toed the stirrup and swung up onto the stallion's back. Emma ran over to where her buckskin was sidling away from the boulders he watched tumble toward him, sounding like a runaway freight train on a steep downhill grade.

The ground was leaping and bounding, pitching like the deck of a storm-tossed ship.

"Come on!" Emma swung the buckskin around,

touched spurs to its flanks, and crouched low over its buffeting mane as the horse lunged off its rear hooves and into an instant gallop.

Wolf needed no prodding from Yakima. Giving a shrill whinny, knowing that the boulders were nearly to the bottom of the canyon wall, the black bolted off its own rear hooves and took off after Emma and the buckskin as though tin cans were tied to its tail. Emma and the buckskin flew into the side canyon, and then Yakima and Wolf were in the side canyon, as well, the half-breed gritting his teeth against the agony every lunging stride evoked in his arm, sending poison-tipped Apache spears of misery shooting all through his battered and bruised body.

By force of will, he turned his heavy head to peer behind him, feeling a cold chill drape itself around him as he saw a large, tan boulder bouncing toward him across the floor of the main canyon. It bounced twice, quickly doubling in size, before slamming into the canyon mouth not fifty feet behind Wolf's lunging hooves. The rock, too large to fit into the mouth—thank God!—had been stopped dead and was now obscured by a thick curtain of dust billowing up around it and even before it, reaching into the smaller canyon toward Yakima.

The dust cloaked him, heavy as a blanket.

The drumming of the boulders tumbling into the

canyon continued, sounding like a massive war played out in heaven. Or maybe hell…

Yakima turned forward with a sigh, shaking his head, blinking against the dust that thinned the farther he rode away from it. "Damn—that was close!"

He sagged forward against Wolf's buffeting mane and slipped into a merciful semi-consciousness. He wasn't sure how much time had passed before the black stopped.

Yakima lifted his head, wincing as the pain in his arm again bit him deep. They were in the open desert. At least it was open to his left. To his right was a tall, wave-shaped escarpment with a concave belly and several boulders at its base. Ahead, near an arroyo cutting around from the far end of the formation, mesquites mixed with tamarisk, greasewood, and ocotillo.

It was still raining, although not as hard as before. The sky was a deep, stormy blue, but the pale-yellow, low-hanging sun brushed it with a clean, lens-like clarity from beneath the western clouds. Thunder rumbled in the distance, but Yakima didn't see lightning. The air was cool and fresh and perfumed with the smell of rain-washed desert, though it didn't appear that much rain had fallen here, wherever they were.

Ahead of Yakima, Emma swung her right boot over her saddle horn and dropped to the ground. She wore a white-and-red checked shirt, a tan Stetson, and blue denims that caressed her curves as lovingly as an appreciative man's hand. The cuffs were stuffed into the tops of her men's brown boots. Her pearl-gripped, 41-caliber New Line Colt bristled on her right hip.

"Where are we?" Yakima asked her as she strode toward him.

"A mile or so from being buried under a few tons of solid rock."

Yakima gave a snarl against the pain in his arm as he swung down from his saddle and turned to her, frowning. "How did you know…?"

"I followed you out from the ranch. Heard the shot. I saw Wolf from a distance dropping into that canyon and followed him." She gave a wan smile. "I figured he was headed for you."

Emma poked her hat brim back off her forehead and inspected his bloody arm. "I can't see a thing through all that blood," she said finally. "How does it feel?"

"As bad as it looks. But I think the bullet missed the bone, or I'd be out by now."

"I have to get it cleaned." Emma looked around, then turned to Yakima once more. "Go sit against that scarp over there. I'll gather wood and build a fire to heat some water."

Yakima grabbed his canteen from over his saddlehorn, popped the cork, and took a long drink and then one more. That made him feel a little better. It fueled him for the short walk to the scarp, anyway.

He shoved the cork back into the flask, hooked the lanyard over his arm, and dragged his boot toes through the brush and boulders to the base of the tall escarpment. He leaned back against the sandstone wall and slid slowly to the ground.

He raised his knees, draped his arms over them, and hung his head. He dozed until he heard her spurs chinking. He lifted his head to see her walking toward him, studying him, frowning with concern, several branches of sun-bleached mesquite in her arms. As she dropped the wood ten feet from where he sat and went to work arranging it for a fire, she glanced up at him.

"Who were they?"

Yakima shook his head. "Bad *hombres*." He didn't have the energy to go into it. He wished he had a flask of whiskey in his saddlebags to dull the pain, but he didn't.

"Why did you follow me?" he asked her later, after he'd dozed again and wakened to find her kneeling beside him, gently cutting the bloody sleeve away from his arm with a folding Barlow knife.

A small fire crackled before them, in a ring of rocks. Emma had heated water, and it steamed now in the small pie pan she'd found in his saddlebags and which he usually used for a plate. Several strips of flannel lay on the ground by the plate. She'd set his coffee pot on the flames, as well. It chugged and hissed softly as the water heated. Nearby lay his sack of Arbuckle's.

It was late afternoon or early evening. Yakima had lost track of time. Shadows had grown long. The storm seemed to have passed. Somewhere, a coyote yammered.

"I know what Poppa threatened you with."

He arched a brow at the girl. "Eavesdropping?"

Emma hiked a shoulder as she soaked the cloth and began gently cleaning the blood from around the wound. She glanced at him and smiled. "I'm a curious girl."

"Did you know about that ace he was holding?"

"The Wanted circular?" Emma nodded. "I saw it several weeks ago. He forgot it on a table in the *salon*. I had a pretty good idea what he was going to use it for." She looked up at Yakima, and her eyes glittered with devious delight. "And, boy, he sure did, all right!"

16

Yakima spat to one side, then sat brooding while Emma cleaned the wound. He almost enjoyed the pain. It was a nice distraction.

"I think you're right," Emma said, when she had the blood washed from his arm. "I think the bullet missed the bone. Might have grazed it. There's an exit hole. The holes'll need to be cauterized."

Yakima's innards recoiled at the term. It sent a chill down his spine. The wound already felt as though it were being cauterized constantly. A big, red heart was throbbing just below his right shoulder.

He pulled the Arkansas toothpick from the sheath behind his neck, held it to her handle first. Emma took it and set the long, tapering blade in the flames.

She gave a sigh and glanced at Yakima again. "Tell me about it. The circular. The lawman you killed."

"Forget it."

"Tell me."

Yakima drew a deep breath and looked off beyond the flames, but he was seeing the main drag of Estelle, Kansas, lit by burning oil pots roughly three years ago. "I didn't even know he was a deputy US marshal." Yakima chuffed ironically at that. "Of all the rotten luck."

"Myers?"

Yakima nodded. "I was on my way down here from up north, stopped for the night in Estelle, little town in western Kansas. Middle of nowhere. After supper I went to a little saloon for a beer and a smoke, and I heard a commotion outside. Stepped out to see a big man tying a smaller man—smaller and younger, nineteen if the kid was that—to a big wagon wheel leaning against a livery barn.

"They were surrounded by several drunk tough nuts egging the big man on. The big man, Myers, grabbed a bullwhip, and he laid into that kid with a vengeance. Through the shouting, and hearing what Myers was sayin' to the kid he was whippin', the kid had whooped him at poker several nights ago. Won a gold watch off him. The kid had been wearing the watch around town. Myers thought he was showin' off, needlin' him. From what I could tell, the kid was a tad on the simple side. I don't think he meant to chafe Myers the way he did.

Anyway, this night Myers was drunk. Dangerous drunk, face all puffed up red, fire in his eyes. He laid into that kid over and over again with the goddamned bullwhip until I couldn't take it anymore. I intervened. Myers drew on me, and I beat him to the punch."

Yakima shook his head. "No one told me his name, let alone his profession. I thought he was just some big, mean no-account. No one seemed all that sad to see him lyin' dead in the street. So, I went back into the saloon, finished my beer, bedded down with Wolf in the livery barn, and rode out of town early the next morning. Hadn't spared a single thought on Myers till your pa showed me that circular in his office."

While he'd told the story, Emma had dumped a handful of ground Arbuckle's into the boiling pot and let it come to a boil again. Now she filled two cups, glancing at Yakima through the fragrant coffee steam. "I'm sorry."

Yakima gave an ironic snort.

"I don't want you to be unhappy," Emma said, sharply. Then her voice lowered, and she frowned. "I guess I'd just rather it was me you were happy with." She blew on her coffee and sipped. "Ironic, isn't it, that he probably wouldn't mind if I was the daughter you were seeing?"

"How's that?"

"I'm a hopeless cause in Poppa's eyes. I'm more boy than girl. He's always said that—the way I ride all over these mountains, critters my only friends, stay outside most of the day. He says I'm out in the sun too much, says no man is going to want a 'boy-wife with an Injun tan and horse muscles.' " She took another sip of her coffee and shook her flaxen hair back from her face. "Besides, Julia's the pretty one. I'm big-boned and ugly. All my life, every man has looked past me to Julia."

"That's just goddamn ridiculous, Emma, and you know it." Yakima's patience was growing thin. He'd assured Emma before that, while Julia was more traditionally beautiful, more the kind of young woman you'd see at a debutante's ball or behind a parlor piano, Emma had a rawer, almost purer beauty all her own. An outdoor beauty. A rugged beauty, but a feminine beauty just the same.

He remembered watching her dance naked in the rain, remembered them making love together with Emma propped on the edge of the well at his old cabin in the Javelina Bluffs, and winced at the old male pull in his loins. It was as though his own body were conspiring with Hugh Kosgrove himself to derail Yakima and Julia's relationship.

"I don't think it's all that ridiculous. After all, you looked past me to Julia… didn't you?"

Guilt flickered in him. He supposed he had, in a way. But his relationship with Emma had been a frivolous affair. An occasional night spent together in the Javelina Bluffs. At least, that's how he'd seen it. He couldn't help it if Emma had seen it as more than that. Besides, when he'd tumbled for Julia, after Lon had been shot in front of them both, he hadn't even known that she was Emma's sister.

"Ah, Jesus," he said, climbing clumsily to his feet. "I can't think about this now. I got bigger fish to fry. I gotta get back to town."

"Hold on, hold on!" Emma stuck her hand in his back pocket and gave it a tug, trying to pull him back down. "I gotta cauterize those wounds, or you'll open up again an' bleed out!"

Yakima resisted her pull. He took a step to one side but grew dizzy and bent forward, resting his hands on his knees.

"See?" Emma said. "You're too weak to ride. You're a good hour from town, Yakima. You'll never make it."

"Ah, Christ." He dropped back down to his butt. He had to get to town, but he was trapped out here by his own weak condition. The men he'd shot in the canyon had been planning a job. He had to assume they were part of a larger group, and that the rest of the group was still planning that job.

His killing the two in the canyon might have delayed the holdup, or whatever it was they were up to. But he couldn't bank on that. He needed to get back to Apache

Springs and help the Kid and Galveston Penny keep a close eye on the town. All three would no doubt be working around the clock for a while.

"Just sit there." Emma climbed to her feet and walked out into the growing darkness beyond the fire, toward their two horses. She returned with a roll of burlap, a smile growing, the low flames reflected in her hazel eyes.

"What's that?"

Emma unwrapped the burlap and, letting the wrap fall to the ground, held up a bottle. "I swiped a bottle of Spanish brandy from Poppa's liquor cabinet."

"What'd you do that for?"

"I hoped to catch up to you. I thought we'd have a drink together... and talk."

"Oh, shit." Yakima had a bad feeling about this. About her. About her and him together. Still, he yearned for a few slugs of that brandy. Nothing like hard liquor for killing the fire in his arm and the aches and pains in assorted other regions of his battered body.

She knelt and handed him the bottle. "Have a couple slugs, and I'll cauterize those wounds."

Yakima looked at her dubiously. She smiled, one eye turning inward, deviously. He took the bottle from her and looked at the Arkansas toothpick resting in the fire. The tapering blade glowed red. He gave a shudder of revulsion, anticipating the raw burn of the blade laid against his already aching arm.

Yakima sighed, popped the cork on the bottle, and took a deep pull.

"Good stuff," he said, though he preferred bourbon. "Won't your father miss it?"

Emma sat back on her butt, knees raised to her chin, watching him. "Nah. He has the stuff hauled in by the case. Never mind he's so cash poor, he can't even afford to pay his own men. He was raised so poor—barefoot poor in the streets of Boston—that he doesn't know a thing about money. About saving it, that is. And spending it wisely."

Yakima took another pull from the bottle. What Emma had just told him about her father being out of cash reminded him of something he'd considered earlier, before he'd been distracted by Hugh Kosgrove's ultimatum.

The Conquistador's payroll was being delivered tomorrow, hauled from the Southern Pacific line by Salko and Kosgrove's other cold-steel men, on their return from delivering the ore. Could the payroll contingent be the "job" Clara had overheard the now-dead bushwhackers discussing in her room?

"Better have one more pull," Emma said, nudging Yakima from his reverie and plucking the hot knife from the fire by its round wooden handle. She held it up before him, grinning malignantly.

"You're enjoying this." Yakima took another deep drink of the brandy, and then one more. He wasn't nearly as worried about the cauterization as he'd been only a few minutes before. The wonder of alcohol. He ran his sleeve across his mouth, then set the bottle between his boots.

"A lover spurned," Emma said, not so vaguely threatening, grinning, staring brashly into Yakima's eyes. She waved the knife in front of his face, then slipped it into her left hand, picked up the bottle with the right one, winked at him with impish deviltry, then took a drink of the brandy.

"You're supposed to be the sober one," Yakima pointed out.

Emma lowered the bottle quickly, choking back a laugh. She pressed her hand against her mouth. Her rich lips were wet, brandy oozing between them, dribbling down her chin. Her eyes were alive, and a beautiful flush shone in her cheeks.

Yakima looked away from her. A byproduct of the alcohol's soothing affect was the tempering of his inhibitions. He was losing his ability to control the feelings—the lust—rising inside him. He'd have to make more of a conscious effort to suppress it.

"Just get on with it."

"Okay, okay, Mister Bossy." Emma set the bottle down between his boots, took the knife in her right hand, scooted around on her knees to his left side. Either inadvertently or not, she brushed her breasts against his forearm. A tingling sensation rippled his lower belly.

He could feel the warmth of her body, smell her sweet sage odor mixing with the fresh smell of the desert after the rain...

"What's takin' so damn long?" he growled, turning to her angrily. "Just do it, will you?"

"It's getting dark out here, I have to get a good look at what I'm doing," Emma said in exasperation. "Jesus!" She took his left hand and laid his arm across her knees. Again, she pressed her breasts against his forearm and held them there as she slid the knife up close to the wound. He looked away, trying to ignore the soft pressure of the tips of her nubile orbs against his bare flesh.

"Here we go," she said. "Ready?"

"Jesus Christ—will you just—ah, *shittttt*!"

As the burn bit him deep, he could smell the nasty odor of his own burning flesh.

"One more!" Emma slid the blade around his arm to the back, then pressed the hot blade over the exit wound.

"Fuck!" Yakima cried through gritted teeth, tensing his jaws and throwing his head straight back to stare up at the kindling stars. As he did, Emma dropped the knife and wrapped fresh flannel strips around the wound. She tied the bandage taut, then lifted the bottle. Yakima took it and

threw back several more swallows, noting that the level in the previously fresh bottle had dropped dramatically.

He could feel the brandy working its spell.

Emma took the bottle back, had a couple of sips, then ran the back of her hand across her mouth.

Yakima lay back and stared at the sky, hearing the flames crackling before him. Emma lay down close beside him, brushing her thumb playfully across his mouth, drawing his lower lip down. The feel of her flesh on his bit him hard. Almost as hard as the bullet.

"How do you feel?"

"Drunk."

"Did your owie go away?" she asked in a little girl's voice—a sexy one, at that.

"Stop talking like that."

She scowled at him, pooching out her lips. "Why are you mad at me? I doctored that wound as well as any sawbones could have done."

The stars swirled above him, making him a little dizzy. "I know what you're doing."

She leaned even closer, staring into his eyes. "What am I doing?"

"You're trying to get my blood up."

Emma laid her hand over the semi-hardness bulging the crotch of his tight denims. Her hand was a soft, hot pressure. He jerked with a start. "Goddamnit, Emma!"

"I'm not sure, kind sir," she said in a mocking sing-song, "but I think your blood is already up. Something else, too, I might add. I think it likes me."

Yakima flicked his right hand, waving her away. "You run along home now. Your old man's gonna get worried."

"He's got a night meeting at the mine. He won't be expecting to see me again till breakfast, if then. We go about our own schedules, Poppa and me. I got all night, Yakima. Just like you do."

He didn't say anything. He just lay staring at the stars, feeling the raw, aching burn diminish by degrees as the alcohol coursed through his veins. He felt better. If it hadn't been for the nettling rake of lust, he'd have felt just fine, albeit drunk.

Emma smoothed his hair back from his forehead, ran her fingers through the long, thick, sweat-damp strands curling behind his ears. Her hands were oddly soothing. In a quiet, intimate voice, she said, "Poppa doesn't make idle threats. It's over between you and Julia. You have to let her go. If he calls the law on you, you'll have to leave or go to jail for a long time. You don't want to leave. This is your home now. Even if there wasn't any consarned bounty on your head, it couldn't work—between you and Julia, I mean. You know it's true. It's just like Poppa said it was. The folks around here would never accept you marryin' up with Hugh Kosgrove's daughter. At least, not his *older* daughter."

Emma smiled. He heard the faint crackle of her saliva as she stretched her lips back from her teeth. "Now, it might just be possible to marry up with his wilder, younger daughter." She reached up and pinched his nose between her thumb and index finger. "No one cares what the Wildcat of the Sierra Estrada does as long as she stays away from the men in town!" She smiled again, impishly. "At least, that's what the women-folk think."

"Go away, Emma. I don't want to talk anymore. I don't want to think anymore. Leave me here. I'll ride back to town when I sober up."

"I don't want to talk anymore, either. But I don't think you want me to go away, Yakima."

Again, her hand pressed warmly down on his bulging crotch. Again, he gave a start.

He lifted his head and glared at her. "Goddamnit, Emma!" His breath caught in his throat. He stared at her. She'd opened her shirt and lifted her chemise off her head. It lay in a frilly white pile beside her. The firelight played across the sides of her full, pale breasts that sloped toward his chest.

Keeping her hand on his crotch, she smiled.

"Yakima!"

The half-breed lifted his head from his saddle with a start.

He blinked, looked around. Had someone called his name, or had he been dreaming?

For a moment, he couldn't remember where he was or what he was doing out here in the desert, flanked by the sandstone outcropping. The fog of pain and alcohol was slow in yielding to consciousness. Then he remembered the bushwhacking, the bullet in his arm, and his tumble into the canyon.

Guilt raked him when he remembered last night, Emma writhing naked beneath him, her long, willowy, buxom body colored Indian-copper in the flames of the dancing fire. Her lips twisted, eyes bright with passion as he bucked against her, between her flapping, wide-spread knees, hardening her jaws and digging her fingers and heels into his back with delight at their rugged coupling.

Oh, shit... Julia...

Now the fire was a small mound of gray ash and bits of charred log in the gray dawn light. The air held a late-summer morning bite. Emma was not around. Her buckskin was not standing near where Wolf stood between two boulders thirty feet away, hobbled and staring off toward Yakima's right, twitching his ears and making a low rumbling deep in his lungs.

Emma must have woken early, gathered her gear while Yakima had slept the sleep of the dead, and ridden quietly off.

"Yakima!"

The half-breed's heart quickened. That was Emma's voice.

It was followed by the distance-muffled belch of a rifle.

Yakima's heart lurched. "Shit..."

He flung his bedroll aside and rose.

"Oh!" His blood plunged to his feet, and a nasty little man with a big hammer banged away inside his head. He stumbled backward on his bare feet, pressing the heels of his hands to his temples. His left arm hurt like a son of a bitch.

Another rifle shot was preceded by the sharp squeal of a bullet off a rock.

Suppressing the countless miseries barking like angry dogs inside him, Yakima stumbled around, gathering his clothes. The blade-like chill portending the desert autumn added to his raging discomfort. Fumbling and stumbling, hearing more rifles crackling somewhere off toward where the sun was lifting its pale head above the eastern ridges, he dressed.

Again, Emma shouted his name. There was no little fear in her voice. Her echoing cry was followed by the hiccup of another rifle.

Quickly deciding that riding would be a faster way of getting to Emma in his still half-drunk and badly battered condition, he hauled his gear out to where Wolf stood, whickering his worry at the shooting and the girl's shouting, and threw the blanket and saddle over the black's back. His scabbard and Yellowboy repeater were strapped securely to the saddle, the rifle's rear stock angling up over the right stirrup. Yakima would leave his saddlebags and blanket roll for now.

He stepped tenderly into the saddle, wincing against the barrage of miseries coursing through him and, holding his tender left arm against his side, touched Wolf's flanks with his spurs.

"Oh, Jesus!" he cried as the horse lunged into a gallop, riling up that demonic little man with the big hammer in his head.

The shooting continued sporadically in the distance, somewhere to the east and south. As Yakima rode, gritting his teeth and crouching low in the saddle, he began to hear the cracks of what sounded like a pistol returning the rifle fire. A small-caliber pistol. Emma's pearl-gripped, .41-caliber New Line Colt.

Yakima and Wolf stormed across the desert, which slowly gained definition as the sun continued to rise, spreading buttery rays across the desert far ahead and beyond some steep, sawtooth ridges. Yakima reined Wolf up and, as the stallion's rear hooves skidded across the sand and gravel, turned to his right.

A steep trail dropped into a canyon to the south. Yakima had seen the trail before. Suddenly, he recognized the rocks and brush around it, as well.

It was the trail into the canyon in which the gold-laden church sat. He hadn't realized he and Emma had been so close to the chasm. This vast mountain desert of the Sierra Estrada looked vastly different from every different angle, and he was far from familiar with it yet. The shooting was coming from the canyon.

"Let's go, boy!"

Yakima reined the stallion down the steep trail that turned sharply to the left at the canyon bottom. Wolf picked his way around rocks and other debris, hugging the canyon's north wall. The wall climbed higher the deeper Wolf and Yakima rode into the canyon, heading southeast toward the church. The sporadic shooting continued, growing louder, until Yakima could see occasional smoke puffs rising from behind rocks ahead of him.

He checked Wolf down in a fringe of mesquites. The horse blew warily, shook its head.

"Easy, easy," Yakima said, running a gloved hand along the mount's left wither.

He stared straight ahead of him, across a field of white rocks and chaparral. Getting the general lay of the land as well as the situation, he urged Wolf ahead once more. The stallion galloped full out, though its rider could feel in the tense muscles beneath the saddle the beast's fear of the flying lead.

Yakima didn't blame him a bit.

Yakima jerked the reins to the right, and, as Wolf swerved in that direction, his rider shucked his Yellowboy from its scabbard and leaped out of the saddle. He yowled as he hit the ground, got his boots tangled, fell, and rolled.

The nasty old man in his head was really going to town now with that hammer. His twin, even nastier brother, was following suit in Yakima's bullet-torn left arm.

The half-breed gave another yelp as he gained his feet. As two bullets plumed dust to his right, he ran ahead and dropped behind a boulder a little higher than a wheelbarrow.

He looked to his right. Emma crouched behind a rock about thirty feet away, looking at him with a haughty expression that said, "It's about time!" Her hat was off, and her hair was tangled. One sleeve of her checked shirt was torn, leaving her shoulder bare. Her buckskin must have thrown her.

Yakima rose with another yelp, and, as two or maybe three rifles cut loose ahead of him, he sprinted across the rough terrain toward Emma. Ten feet away from her covering boulder, a bullet nipped his left pants cuff. Again, he dropped and then rolled up against Emma's boulder, breathing hard and sweating. He'd lost his hat in the roll, and now he slid his own tangled hair back from his face and turned to the girl.

"What the hell's goin' on?"

"What's it look like?" Emma said in fiery exasperation, holding her pearl-gripped Colt barrel up in her right, gloved hand. "Some nasty sons of bitches have found the church!" Her eyes blazed wickedly, as though somehow this was his fault. "I told you this would happen!"

"Well, I didn't do it!"

"I don't think you have any idea what this means!" She was talking about the Apache curse.

"Like I said, I didn't leave no trail of bread crumbs for anyone to follow into your precious canyon." Yakima drew his head down lower behind the boulder as a bullet smashed into the other side of it. He looked at Emma again, concern in his gaze. "Are you all right?"

"They fired on me. The buckskin pitched an' threw me. The bushwhacking sonso'bitches!"

Emma jerked her head up above the boulder and triggered two quick rounds at the bushwhackers.

"Keep your head down," Yakima scolded her. "That pea-shooter of yours isn't going to do a damn thing from this distance except get you killed!"

Emma flicked open the Colt's loading gate and shook spent cartridges onto the ground beside her. "What are we gonna do? Those shooters obviously don't like us being down here in this canyon any better than I want them carrying off that treasure."

Yakima didn't know what to believe about the curse. What he believed or didn't believe about the witch's hex didn't matter. Obviously, the three men shooting at him and Emma didn't intend to let them leave the canyon alive. They'd likely discovered the treasure and didn't much care for the idea of sharing.

Yakima turned onto his right shoulder and edged a look around the rock. One of the shooters, outlined against the sun rising up from behind the canyon's eastern wall, was just then running up toward Yakima and Emma, tracing a zigzag pattern through the chaparral and holding an old Winchester rifle up high across his chest. He appeared dark-skinned, and he wore a cream shirt and suspenders, a palm-leaf *sombrero* topping his head.

Yakima aimed quickly and fired, but his bullet merely blew up dirt and gravel as the man dropped behind another boulder a dozen or so yards to Yakima's left, maybe half that many yards ahead of his and Emma's position.

Too damned close for comfort. Out of the corner of his right eye, the half-breed spied more movement and turned to see another man running toward the arroyo on his and Emma's right.

"Goddamnit," Yakima bit out. "They're tryin' to get us in a whipsaw!"

Yakima swung his Yellowboy around and fired over Emma's head at the man to the south. The half-breed couldn't see the bastard, but only the brush and rocks he'd gone to ground in. He just wanted to discourage any more crowding, hold them off for as long as possible.

Yakima had just ejected the spent, smoking cartridge and pumped another one into the Yellowboy's action when another lurch of sudden movement drew his gaze straight out before him. The third man was running straight up toward Yakima's position, weaving between mesquites and boulders. Quickly, Yakima aimed and fired. The slug blew rock dust from a boulder far beyond where the man had just swerved behind a stout barrel cactus.

A rifle cracked in the distance down-canyon, in the direction of the treasure-laden church. Yakima stared toward it, a butterfly of dread flapping its wings against the back of his neck.

As if the three bushwhackers working their way around him and Emma weren't enough, there was a fourth shooter!

The thought had just passed through Yakima's brain when deep lines of incredulity cut across his forehead as he watched the third man stumble out from behind the barrel cactus. The shooter staggered to one side as though drunk. His bowler hat tumbled off his shoulder. His rifle slipped from his gloved hands to clatter on the rocks around his high-topped, mule-eared boots. He fell to his knees and then to his face and lay still. Blood glistened up high on his back.

Yakima and Emma shared a look.

What the hell?

Yakima whipped around toward the man standing behind the boulder on his left. The man was aiming his rifle at him, from over the top of his covering rock. The man's head jerked violently to one side as smoke and flames lapped from his Winchester's barrel. The bullet sizzled through the air over Yakima's head to spang off a distant rock.

The shooter fell forward, head lolling on his shoulders as though his neck were little more than a thread. He fell forward, on top of his rifle, and lay still.

He, too, had been shot from behind.

Yakima glanced over his and Emma's boulder, staring off down the canyon. Smoke puffed from a low pinnacle of eroded rock about fifty yards away. At almost the same time, the man in the arroyo, hidden by wiry shrubs on an island in the arroyo's center, screamed shrilly. From that same island, a rifle thundered, flames lancing out of the brush to the east, in the direction of the fourth shooter.

The distant shooter fired again, smoke puffing from the same spot as before on the finger of rock.

Again, the man in the arroyo screamed.

Another hit.

There was a wild crunching of brush, and then the man appeared, staggering out of the thicket, grunting and wheezing. He dropped his rifle, ran a few more steps before getting his boots entangled. Then he dropped and crawled a few more feet on all fours before collapsing. Blood spotted his light-blue work shirt between his shoulder blades.

Emma stared at the man in the arroyo. Slowly, she turned her head toward Yakima, eyes cast with wonder.

The half-breed shrugged. Slowly, he rose as he stared off toward the finger of rock. No movement over there now. Yakima shouldered his rifle and stepped out around the boulder, walking slowly down-canyon, head canted to one side, eyes narrowed in wary curiosity.

He stopped when a horse trotted out from behind the finger of rock. A wide-shouldered, heavy-set gent rode toward Yakima and Emma, who'd just stepped up to the half-breed's right, staring after the big man riding toward them on a beefy sorrel with a spray of white spots across its withers and chest.

Something shiny was pinned to the newcomer's vest.

"Well, I'll be hanged," Yakima said.

The Rio Grande Kid continued riding toward them, head canted to one side.

18

The Rio Grande Kid brought the sorrel up to within ten feet of Yakima and Emma and checked it down. The Kid didn't look happy. In fact, he looked vexed as hell as he said with uncustomary formality, "You okay, Marshal Henry? Miss Emma?"

Emma's cheeks colored, and her jaws hardened angrily. "Don't 'Marshal Henry' him and don't 'Miss Emma' me, you old outlaw. How did you know about this canyon?" She'd spat the words out like four-letter epithets, leaning slightly forward at her waist, gloved hands bunched at her sides.

"How'd *you* know about it?" the Kid returned in an indignant tone.

"I've known about it for years!"

"It's her canyon," Yakima said, canting his head toward Emma. "Leastways, that's how she sees it."

Emma opened her mouth to offer a bitter retort, but Yakima held up his hand, cutting her off. He kept his curious gaze on the Kid. "What're you doing out here?" He glanced at the dead man lying in the gravel by the barrel cactus, adding, "Not that I mind, mind you, but…"

"When you didn't come back to town last night, I decided to ride out and have a look. Galveston can keep the lid on the town on a weeknight. I rode out to the Conquistador, talked to a coupla ornery characters ridin' roughshod along the place's perimeter. They told me you left hours ago, so I headed back this way. It was too dark to track you, so I decided to hole up at the old church back yonder"—he gave Emma a sour, suspicious glance before returning his gaze to Yakima—"and wait till daylight to continue lookin'. Heard the shootin' come first light, and Miss Emma yellin' your name."

"You spent the night at the church?" Emma said.

"That's what I said, Miss Kosgrove."

"Don't 'Miss Kosgrove' me, you old outlaw. How did you know about the church?"

Before the Kid could respond to the girl's question, Yakima smiled knowingly and said, "You didn't lose that map out of your Bible, did you? You just put it away for safe keeping."

The Kid puffed up his lumpy chest as he sighed. "I realized how valuable it was"—again he cut his defensive gaze at Emma—"after it finally brought me to this canyon about three months ago." Keeping his eyes on Emma, he said, "How did you say you knew about it?"

"Never mind," Yakima said. "Who're these fellas?"

"Hell if I know," the Kid said. "I just seen 'em slingin' lead at you and Miss Kosgrove. I recognized you when you galloped in on Wolf. So I climbed up that rock there—damn near fell an' broke my neck, don't ya know!—and lined up the sights on 'em." He ran an appreciative hand down his Spencer repeater. "Not bad shootin' for an old catamount—would you say, Yak?"

"Not bad for an old catamount," Yakima agreed.

The Kid winced and shook his head as he studied the dead man by the barrel cactus. "Last night I saw that someone had been here and found the church. There's the remains of a recent campfire out front of it. These three drygulchers must've found the canyon on a previous trip an' were comin' back this mornin' to start packin' out the treasure, gallblast their hides anyways!"

He hooked a thick thumb over his shoulder. "I seen their horses back yonder—an' three mules outfitted with pack frames and *aparejos*."

"Shit!" Emma said. "This is terrible!"

"I'll say it's terrible!" the Kid complained, slapping his battered, weather-stained hat against his canvas-clad thigh, causing dust to waft. "Here I thought I found the mother lode of riches all by my lonesome. Wasn't gonna have to share it with nobody. I thought I was gonna be richer than a half-dozen Jay Goulds for the first and last time in my life. Hell, I was gonna go down to Mexico and find me a whorehouse an'…" His gaze fell on Emma, and his ears turned pink. "Oh… never mind…"

Emma stomped up close to the potbellied Kid and looked up at him pointedly, narrowing one eye suspiciously. "Did you take anything out of that church? Any ingots or anything in the box atop the altar?"

"Not yet," the Kid said, curling his upper lip and flaring one nostril defiantly. "I thought it might be safer right where it was… till I could think of a way to haul it out of there without raising suspicion." He canted his head to one side and returned Emma's suspicion-slitted stare. "How 'bout you? Did you take anything out o' that church?"

"I certainly did not, and you can't, either. Not ever! And you can't tell a single soul about what's down here in this canyon." Emma trotted around Yakima and the Rio Grande Kid and strode over to where the dead man lay by the barrel cactus. She kicked him over on his back, slid a lock of hair back from her cheek, and stared down at the dead man. "Oh, no."

Yakima had just whistled for Wolf. He'd spent enough time in the canyon. His focus now was on getting to

Kosgrove's riders before they were hit for the payroll they were carrying back to the Conquistador from the Southern Pacific tracks. But now, waiting for the stallion, he turned to Emma. "What is it?"

Emma turned to him and pointed at the dead man at her feet. "This is one of my father's men."

"Sure enough?" said the Kid.

Emma ran over to the second man the Kid had shot. "This one, too."

She ran into the arroyo and kicked the third man over on his back. She looked up again at Yakima. "This one's name is Hale. I don't know the others, but I recognize them. They're professional packers. They ride with Poppa when he goes off deeper into the mountains looking for gold-rich quartz veins."

"You think your father knows about this canyon?" Yakima asked, hearing Wolf's hooves drumming behind him.

"Ah, hell," the Kid lamented, again slapping his hat across his thigh, causing even more dust to billow. "Who *doesn't* know about it?"

Ignoring the stout deputy, Emma kept her eyes on Yakima. "I don't know. Maybe they found it on their own." She turned slowly to stare curiously, darkly down at the man lying dead at her boots. "Maybe not..."

Yakima grabbed his reins and swung up onto Wolf's back, wincing again at the pain the maneuver sent through him in waves. This excursion into the canyon hadn't done his condition any good at all, but he didn't think his arm had opened up again.

"Where are you going?" Emma asked.

"Yeah, where you goin', Yak?" the Kid echoed.

"I think I know what job those two bastards from Señora Galvez's place were talking about. Those two are buzzard bait, but I'm thinking they were part of a larger group. And I'm thinking that larger group is fixing to hit the Kosgrove payroll on its way back from the Southern Pacific tracks. Fetch your horse, Kid. We got work to do!"

"Work?" The Kid stared at him, hang-jawed, astounded. "How can you think of *work* when there's all that gold back there! We gotta get it out! We gotta get it out right now before others get onto it!"

"Oh, no you don't!" Emma drew her Colt. She climbed up out of the arroyo, looking as mad as a peeled rattlesnake, and stood glaring and aiming the pistol at the Kid. "You try to take one trinket out of that church, and I'll fill you so full of lead you'll rattle when you walk, old man!"

"Ah, Christ!" Yakima reined Wolf around and spurred him back down the canyon.

He was halfway back to Apache Springs when, after slowing Wolf from a lope to rest him, he heard hoof thuds growing louder behind him. He reached for the Colt holstered on his right thigh but stayed the motion when he saw that the two approaching riders were none other than the Kid and Emma. They looked as owly as two school kids after a nasty dustup behind a buggy shed.

The Kid checked his mount at Yakima's left stirrup, matching Yakima's pace. Emma checked her buckskin at his right stirrup, also matching the half-breed's pace.

"I was listening for gunfire," Yakima said, "thinking you two might shoot each other back yonder. It's a wonder what gold will do to a person."

"We came to an agreement," the Kid said tightly, staring straight over his horse's twitching ears.

"Well?" Yakima said when neither one elaborated.

"We agreed that I wouldn't shoot him if he left that gold alone," Emma said, looking past Yakima at her newly minted nemesis, the Kid.

The Kid turned to Yakima; his eyes indignant beneath the brim of his battered Stetson. "I think she woulda done it, just like she said. She woulda gut-shot me an' left me there to bloat up an' rot with her old man's gun wolves!"

Emma winked at him. "My trigger finger is still itchin'."

The Kid said to Yakima, "She's purtier'n a speckled pup, Miss Emma is. But I've come to believe she's mean-er'n a back-alley cur with fourteen sucking pups!"

"When it comes to that gold, you better believe it," Emma agreed.

"What's the plan?" Yakima asked her. "You going to

hound-dog him for the rest of his days to make sure he doesn't ride back out to that canyon?"

"If that's what it takes."

"What about you, Yak?" The Kid studied the half-breed lawman, puzzled. "Don't you want none o' that gold?"

"Nope."

"How come?"

Yakima hiked a shoulder. "Believe me, when I first saw that church, I felt the fever. But how would you ever get that treasure out of that canyon without every seedy-eyed border snake in Arizona getting word and running out here to 'help'? No one could ever be satisfied with only an ingot or two. You'd want the works, or you'd never sleep at night."

He spat over the side of his saddle and chuckled. "Anyone tries hauling that gold out of that canyon is going to go up against an army of desperadoes intent on relieving them of it. Shit, there'll likely be a war that'll make the Misunderstanding Between the States look like a game of schoolyard kickball. Besides, look what that gold has done to you two."

Yakima looked from the Kid on his left to Emma on his right. "An upstanding deputy town marshal and Hugh Kosgrove's purty, polite daughter goin' at each other like a wolf and a mountain lion trapped in the same privy. You two oughta be ashamed of yourselves."

"It's not the gold I'm after," Emma said, defensively. "What I'm after is keeping it where it belongs!"

"What do you think, Yak?" the Kid said after they'd ridden in silence for a while, the sun really burning down on them now at nearly midday, not a shadow in sight. "Do you believe that gold is really cursed like this purty wildcat says it is?"

"From the trouble I've seen it cause so far?" Yakima said, raking his gaze again between his two trail partners. "Hell, yes, I do!"

The Kid glowered, sheepish. Emma did the same.

"Say," the Kid said after another brief silence, "were you two together out here last night?"

Now it was Yakima's ears that turned red. He cut his eyes at Emma, who smiled at him lustily. "Oh, yes," she said. "We certainly were."

Guilt battered Yakima nearly as badly as his tumble down the canyon wall.

"Could we stop all this consarned chinnin'?" He raked spurs against Wolf's flanks, urging the black into a gallop. "I got a job to do!"

19

Yakima rode into Apache Springs around one o'clock in the afternoon.

He weaved Wolf through the early afternoon traffic, of which there was getting to be more and more. As he drew up to the town marshal's office, he saw Galveston Penny another block to the west, helping an old, gray-bearded prospector—of whom there were also getting to be more and more around here lately—wrestle a shod wheel onto the oldster's rickety-looking farm wagon while the mule in the traces craned its head around to watch and offer comment in the form of an occasional bray.

Around them, shoppers and shopkeepers and other businessmen milled. Hooves thudded, and the wheels of wagons and buggies creaked and clattered. A low din rose, comprised of those sounds, as well as the conversations of men and women on the street and on the boardwalks, and of the painted young ladies lounging or flouncing on several second-floor balconies or leaning over the balcony rails, trying to drum up business on the street below.

Yakima waved his hat at the young deputy, letting him know he and the Kid were back in town. Penny returned the gesture, then continued helping the prospector. The Kid drew up to the jailhouse behind Yakima. Emma rode up beside the half-breed lawman, sidled the buckskin up close to Wolf, turned to Yakima with a sultry smile, then reached out to flick some dust from his cheek, letting her gloved hand linger on his shoulder.

"Buy a thirsty girl a drink?"

Yakima grabbed her hand and squeezed it, not with affection but annoyance. "Like I said, I have a job to do, and you need to get one thing…"

He let the words trail to a stop when his office door latch clicked. He turned to see Julia step out of the office clad in a ruffle-fronted, light-yellow day dress with small feathered hat pinned to her piled, glistening brown hair. A matching reticule hung from her right wrist. As she drew the door closed behind her, she looked forward to see Yakima sitting Wolf by the hitch rack, and a smile of unabashed delight began to lighten her gray eyes and draw her lips away from her teeth.

But then she saw Yakima holding the hand of none other than her younger sister, who sat her horse uncommonly close to his own—so close that their thighs were pressed taut against each other—and Julia's smile faded as quickly as it had arisen.

Emma's voice was toneless as she said, "Oh... oh."

Yakima froze. He looked down to see Emma's hand in his, their legs touching.

He looked up again at Julia, who stood on the gallery, her face now ashen with shock as she slid her gaze between Yakima and Emma, then back again.

Yakima drew a breath and let it out slowly, saying, "Julia..."

He couldn't continue. He wasn't sure how.

Behind Yakima, he vaguely heard the Kid breathe out a hushed, "Oh... shit..."

Yakima tried again. "Julia—"

She cut him off by shaking her head. "Don't say anything." She looked at him and then at Emma once more, her eyes becoming two cold, gray stones at the bottom of a shallow stream, and shook her head again. "There's no need."

She placed her hand on the gallery rail and carefully trod down the three steps to the street. She did not look at Yakima or Emma again but kept her eyes lowered as she hurried off down the street to the east. She glanced over her left shoulder, waiting for a break in the traffic. When one came, she crossed Main Street and disappeared down Third Avenue toward her house.

Yakima turned to Emma. She stared down at her saddle horn.

"Happy, now?" he asked her.

She turned to him. He was surprised that she didn't look happy or even satisfied. She looked sad.

Quietly, she said, "You underestimate me, Yakima."

She backed the buckskin away from the hitch rack, then turned the mount and gigged it westward along Main Street, threading her way through traffic. She was probably heading for a livery barn to put up her horse. Her father owned a hotel on the west side of town, The Conquistador Inn, and she'd probably spend the night there before heading back to the Conquistador in the morning. A livery stable for hotel patrons flanked the large, three-story building outfitted with a tony saloon.

Yakima watched her ride away. As he did, the Kid put his sorrel up beside him.

"Uh... sorry about that... Yakima." The older man brushed a sheepish fist across his mouth and sighed, looking away.

Yakima swung down from the saddle and handed his reins to the Kid. "Take our horses to the Federated, will you? Pick out a couple of good fresh ones. We'd best get started south and see about Kosgrove's payroll."

"You got it."

When the Kid was gone, Yakima climbed the gallery steps, then turned to look off toward where Julia had disappeared. A rusty knife of loss stabbed his belly, twisting.

He'd loved another one, and he'd lost another one. It was probably best for Julia that it had happened this way. He'd decided to break it off with her despite how desperately he didn't want to. The Wanted dodger really had very little to do with it. What Kosgrove had said before he'd pulled that ace out of his sleeve had convinced the lawman that the man was right, although he hadn't realized it until just a while ago, when he'd been riding back to town.

What kind of future would they have had—him and Julia? Marriage? Kids—*Kosgrove's half-breed grandchildren?* The town would shut down around Julia and those kids, and Yakima couldn't put her through it. He could have taken her away from here, he supposed. But her family was here. Her roots were here.

Besides, Yakima was a drifter. Julia was not. She was not like Faith. Faith had hit bottom before she'd met Yakima, and he'd picked her up on his own rebound from his own bottom. Faith could have been happy anywhere, as long as she and Yakima were together. That wouldn't hold true for Julia. She was more delicate than Faith was. She needed stability. She was bound here in Apache Springs, where her father could take care of her until she found another man.

The right man.

The knife twisted a little more.

Feeling wobbly on his feet, Yakima went into the office and pegged his hat by the door. He found a bottle amongst the Kid's gear, took it over to his desk, and slacked into his chair. As he plucked the cork from the bottle with his teeth, he looked down at his desk. His heart thudded, and the knife in his belly twisted again.

She'd left a note for him on a lined tablet. She'd left the tablet in the middle of the desk, facing him, so that he'd be sure to see it. In her pretty, feminine writing, it read:

Dearest Yakima,

I hope you've made it back safely. If you can spare an hour or two... or three... please stop by the house for a meal. I'm sure you're famished, and you need to eat. Besides, I yearn to feast my eyes again on your handsome face.

All my love,

Your Julia.

"Goddamnit to hell!"

He raked the note from the tablet, wadded it up in both hands, and tossed it into a wastebasket. He pushed his chair out and leaned forward, elbows on his knees, and raked his hands back through his long, sweaty, trail-dusty hair.

"Goddamnit to Christ!"

For several seconds he felt as though he would vomit. Finally, he sat back in the chair. He looked at the whiskey bottle. He'd been going to use the whiskey to clean his bullet-torn arm. Now he didn't care about that. He needed the whiskey more on the inside, to quell the ache in his heart, the dull rusty knife in his belly. He plucked the bottle off the desk and took several deep swallows.

He set the bottle back down on the desk, brushed his sleeve across his mouth. He didn't feel any better than before the drink. He looked out a front window. The Kid was riding up to the jailhouse on a broad-barreled bay. He was trailing a light-footed blue roan. Yakima lifted the bottle again, took another couple of deep swallows.

Those eased the aches and pains in his battered bones and muscles, but they did nothing to remove the knife from his belly. In fact, he thought the blade had become even duller and rustier.

He rose with a curse, stomped wearily over to the door, grabbed his hat, and went out.

"You look like death warmed over," the Kid said from atop his rented bay. "Maybe you better let me an' Galveston ride out to meet the payroll train."

"You'd like that, wouldn't you, you old bandit?" Yakima swung up onto the roan's back and grinned at his beefy deputy. "Then you could rob those riders yourself and be in Mexico by morning."

"Damn," the Kid said, scowling. "You must be able to see right through me!"

Yakima turned the roan out into the street. He rode over to where Galveston Penny was just then tightening the hub on the prospector's wagon while the prospector leaned against a *ramada* post, drinking from a clay jug.

"The Kid and I are heading out again," Yakima told Penny. "We're going to meet Kosgrove's payroll train."

Penny brushed wheel dope from his hands on the side of the prospector's wagon, which was loaded with mining implements and feed for the oldster's mule. "You think it's gonna get hit?"

"I think there's a good chance. In the meantime, keep a sharp eye out around here. The bank *might* be the target, but I'm thinkin' it's the payroll."

"Don't worry, Marshal Henry," young Penny said, picking up his Winchester carbine from where it leaned against the wagon. "I'll keep these peepers peeled!"

"You stay away from Señora Galvez's place," the Kid warned him, leaning forward against his saddle horn.

Galveston Penny flushed. The old prospector spat out a mouthful of who-hit-John, laughing.

Yakima swung the roan back into the street and gigged it west. The Kid riding off his right stirrup, he galloped on out of town and up the rise to the pass through the red rocks of a dyke that curved down over the shoulder of the mountain, like the spine of a half-buried stone dinosaur.

He beat it down the other side of the pass, then leveled out on the desert below, following the old stage and mail road west. Then he turned south through chaparral-bristling desert, the dark humps of purple mountains surrounding him in every direction, the Sierra Estrada and the Chiricahuas now flanking him.

He and the Kid dipped down through a broad, flat-bottomed arroyo paved with black volcanic rock still damp from a recent gully washer and then climbed a knoll on the other side. Atop the knoll, they checked their mounts. Yakima stared along the trail before him.

A black mass of wagons and outriders lay roughly a mile ahead.

"That must be them," Yakima said. Just before touching spurs to the roan's flanks, he cast a habitual glance over his right shoulder. Someone was riding up behind them—a rider coming fast, tan dust rising from the galloping hooves of Emma's horse. It was her, all right. Yakima could pick that succulent figure and dancing flaxen hair out of a crowd of any size.

Goddamn her!

"What the hell are you doing?" he asked her as she drew rein before him and the Kid, her dust billowing over all three of them.

Emma tossed her hair back defiantly. "It's my father's payroll that might be hit. That makes it *my* payroll, too."

Yakima shook his head. "Nope. Get back to town. First

thing in the morning, you ride back to the Conquistador."

Emma scowled, puzzled. "Why do you care about the Conquistador payroll? After that stunt my father pulled."

"It's my job," Yakima said, leaning forward in the saddle, his dark eyes grave. "Go on home!"

Emma said softly but pragmatically, "It had to end one way or another, Yakima. This way it's a clean break."

Frustration as well as embarrassment burned in his cheeks. He glanced at the Kid, who was tactfully looking away while fidgeting around as though ants had invaded his saddle.

"Christ!" was all Yakima could think of to say.

He reined the roan around and galloped on down the hill toward the shadowy column lumbering toward him beneath a tan dust cloud. He felt eyes on him and turned to see the Kid, galloping off his right stirrup, staring at him incredulously. The Kid looked away.

"What?" the half-breed said, peeved.

"Nothin'," the Kid said, the wind bending his hat brim back against the crown. "I was just thinkin' to myself that there goes a fella with a complicated life!"

"Yeah, well, it's about to get a lot less complicated," Yakima grumbled, sliding his eyes to one side. Emma followed close behind him, lips pursed with customary defiance. He didn't look at her closely, but he thought he glimpsed a faint smile in her feral blue eyes.

Yakima and the Rio Grande Kid rounded a bend in the trail and continued straight toward the wagon train.

Two men rode out front of the train, maybe a hundred yards from the train's first wagon. Two more men rode about fifty yards behind the first two outriders. Yakima spied more outriders to each side of the train, weaving their way through the chaparral, on guard for a possible attack.

When Yakima was roughly fifty yards from the first two outriders, he saw both men tense and raise their rifles.

"Let's hold up here," Yakima yelled to the Kid and Emma and checked the roan.

The first two outriders glanced at each other. One turned his head as though to issue orders to the other men behind him, and then he and his partner kicked their horses into rocking gallops, intent on checking out the newcomers for possible threat.

When they were halfway between Yakima's group and the other two riders behind them, they slowed and walked their horses up to Yakima's threesome. Both men held their rifles up high across their chests. The half-breed lawman could see that the hammers of both rifles were rocked back to full cock.

"Easy, easy," he said when he saw that the rider on the left was Jake Salko, the contingent's ramrod.

Salko jerked the red bandanna from over his nose and mouth and, glancing at the five-pointed stars winking on both Yakima's and the Kid's chests, and seeing Emma Kosgrove flanking the lawmen, stitched his dusty eyebrows curiously beneath the broad brim of his hat.

Yakima said, "Any trouble, Salko?"

"No," the man said, glancing skeptically at his partner scowling beside him. "Why do you ask, Henry?"

"We got word in town that someone's fixing to pull a job of some kind. I thought it might be Kosgrove's payroll."

Salko canted his head warily to one side. "How did you know I was haulin' payroll?"

"Kosgrove." Yakima raked a thumb down his cheek. "Thought I'd check it out."

"Well, we ain't hit trouble so far…"

Yakima glanced at the Kid, who arched a puzzled brow.

Yakima turned to Salko. "Who all knows when Kosgrove's going to haul his payroll up from the Southern Pacific?"

"Just me and the other men in my crew. Hell, I don't even know when I'll be haulin' payroll till the night before we leave the Conquistador with a load of ore."

Yakima pondered the information.

Salko pursed his lips and shook his head. "I think you're barkin' up the wrong tree, Henry. There's no way anyone outside of my men with me now could know that we're hauling payroll. I'm surprised Mister Kosgrove even mentioned it to you. He runs a pretty tight ship, Kosgrove does."

Yakima saw no need to inform the ramrod he'd only overheard Kosgrove speaking about the payroll to his mine superintendent. He looked behind Salko and Salko's partner. The other two forward outriders had stopped their horses about fifty yards away. The wagon train was also stopped on the two-track trail, weaving its way through the desert rocks and scrub.

Yakima looked around warily. He'd kept a close eye on both sides of the trail out of Apache Springs and hadn't spied anything suspicious.

Salko said, "Like I said, I think you got it wrong, Henry. Now, if you wouldn't mind stepping aside, we're late gettin' back as it is. We lost a wheel rim only a few miles north of the tracks, and two mules threw their shoes at almost the same time. We won't be getting back to the Conquistador till late."

"Yeah, I probably have it wrong." Yakima studied the man riding beside Salko and then glanced back at the others. Two of the other outriders just now rode out of the chaparral to rein their mounts to a stop on the trail behind Salko and his partner and stared curiously at Yakima's group and their foreman.

"Everything all right, Jake?" one of them asked after pulling his bandanna down from over his nose and mouth. He was holding a double-barreled shotgun, and his left cheek bulged with chaw.

Salko glanced behind him. "Tell the drivers to come on—we're rollin'!" He turned back to Yakima, brows ridged impatiently. "Well, Henry?"

Both men behind Salko beckoned to the wagons.

Yakima could hear the mule skinners popping their blacksnakes over their teams as the big ore wagons rocked into forward motion. One of the mules brayed. The mule skinners yelled, whistled, and cursed. The wagons clattered loudly over chuckholes.

"Any new men on the crew?" Yakima asked Salko.

Salko studied him, his brows stitching more tightly, forming an upside down V between his eyes. He glanced at the man riding to his left—a fair-skinned gent with a badly sunburned and peeling nose. Rust-red hair dropped from the man's Stetson, which wore a bullet hole in a corner of its crown, right up along the crease.

"Yeah, we got a few greenhorns," Salko said. "It's the kinda job a fella stays with till somethin' better comes along. That usually don't take long." He turned back to Yakima. "You think…?"

"How many new men on your roll here, Salko?"

"Five. Er, six, I mean." Again, Salko glanced at the man to his left. "All in one new bunch," he added, studying the rusty-headed man with sudden gravity. "Including you—ain't that right, Clavin?"

"That's right," Clavin said, staring hard at Yakima. "What's your beef with new men, breed? Me an' my pards got cut loose from a ranch that went under up north, on the rim. We needed work, so our boss wrote us a recommendation to Mister Kosgrove, and he was good enough to hire six capable outriders."

"Who was your boss?" Yakima said. "This rim rancher."

"Benson." Clavin spoke the name tightly, adding just as tightly, "Why?"

To Salko, Yakima said, "Do you know a rancher named Benson up on the rim? I used to have a ranch near Bailey Peak, and I never heard of any Benson up that way."

"So, what are you sayin' breed? Chew it up a little finer."

"A young whore in town recognized two men from the bunch that attacked and burned Apache Springs nearly two years ago. There were six men of the bunch who got away. I figure they went down to Mexico. They might have returned by now, gained a couple more men, and headed this way to kill me and make another play. They would have known about the Conquistador from their now-dead leader, Rebel Wilkes, who was once a mining engineer for Kosgrove.

"The two men the whore recognized are lying dead in a canyon back in the Sierra Estrada. I figure they were trying to trim my wick to keep me from spoiling the new game they and the rest of their bunch found to play around here." Yakima paused and stared hard at Clavin. "Ain't that right, Clav—?"

He didn't have time to finish the sentence. Clavin's hands became a blur as he suddenly raised his Winchester, swinging it toward Salko. The carbine thundered and stabbed flames toward the foreman, who jerked back in his saddle as his pinto squealed and pitched.

"Take 'em, boys! Take 'em!" the wild-eyed Clavin bellowed as he swung the Winchester toward Yakima, whose horn-gripped Colt came up quickly and roared.

His bullet took Clavin in the shoulder, causing the man's own shot to sail past Yakima's right ear. Clavin bellowed and sawed back on the reins of his own pitching mount. He tried to level his rifle again, but he didn't get another bullet off before the lawman's Colt bucked twice more, blowing Clavin back over the arched tail of his pitching horse, which kicked his left shoulder as he hit the ground.

Yakima held his rented horse's reins taught as he punched a killing shot through the howling man's left ear.

The thunder of a wagon grew louder behind Yakima. Pistols popped, and rifles belched loudly, men shouting and screaming as the robbers who'd infiltrated Kosgrove's guards began shooting the others. Yakima swung the roan around and was about to kick it back toward the wagons but stopped when Emma shouted, "Yakima!"

He jerked his head toward where she and the Kid sat their horses behind him, staring toward four riders galloping toward them from the direction of town. The four had rifles raised to their shoulders, their reins in their teeth. Smoke puffed from the maws of their rifles, bullets kicking up dust around Yakima's, the Kid's, and Emma's prancing mounts.

The Kid turned his anxious gaze to Yakima. "They're tryin' to get us in a whipsaw!"

Yakima punched his Colt into its holster, shucked his Yellowboy from its scabbard, and swung down from his saddle. The Kid did likewise as Emma dropped smoothly off her buckskin's back.

As the roan and the other horses ran off, buck kicking, Yakima dropped to a knee and levered a cartridge into his Winchester's chamber. He stared at the four riders hammering toward him. He'd have bet gold ingots to goose eggs that those four had been waiting for the payroll contingent in the broad arroyo he'd crossed half a mile back. That's where they'd intended to cut down the legitimate guards and take the payroll, probably turn the wagons south along the arroyo paved with black rock before transferring the money to mules and heading south to Mexico.

Bullets chopped the chaparral on both sides of the trail. They plunked into the dirt around Yakima, the Kid, and Emma and spanged off rocks.

Quickly, Yakima dropped belly down. The Kid followed suit to his left, Emma to his right, extending her New Line Colt and thumbing the hammer back.

Yakima centered a bead on one of the fast-approaching riders, squeezed the Yellowboy's trigger, and watched with satisfaction as the rider jerked backward and sideways in his saddle, drawing his reins back so quickly that both he and his horse went down in a thick, churning cloud of bright-red dust. Yakima quickly fired again and again, until all five horses were galloping off into the chaparral on both sides of the trail, their riders rolling in the dirt behind them.

He hadn't realized the Kid and Emma had moved away from him until they shouted his name at the same time, their voices nearly drowned by a hammering, near-deafening thunder.

"Get off the trail!" the Kid wailed.

Yakima jerked a look behind him. A four-hitch team of sweat-lathered mules was bearing down on him fast, foam from their open mouths whipping from their leathery snouts. The ground vibrated. There were two men in the driver's box. One was whipping a blacksnake over the team's backs. The other stood with a Winchester raised to his shoulder. He was aiming over the front of the team at Yakima sprawled in the trail's dead center.

"Yakima, get out of the way!" Emma screamed.

Yakima hurled himself off the trail just as the lead mules' scissoring hooves were about to rip him to shreds. A rifle thundered, though it sounded little louder than a derringer above the team and wagon's roar.

The bullet tore across the outside of Yakima's right ear as he rolled into the brush. When he looked up, squinting against his own swirling dust and that of the wagon's large, churning wheels, the man with the rifle turned quickly, tracking him.

Yakima snapped up the Yellowboy and fired three times quickly, punching the shooter over the driver and out of sight down the wagon's far side. As the wagon flew past, Yakima dropped his rifle, leaped to his feet, and, reacting more than thinking, took off at a dead run.

He leaped up and grabbed the top of the wagon's rear wooden gate. Grunting and groaning and running along behind the wagon, he hoisted himself up and over the gate. He dropped into the wagon, hitting the floor of the box with an indignant groan.

A steel-banded strongbox containing Kosgrove's mine payroll was fixed to the box's middle by stout log chains hooked to rings in each of the wagon's four corners. Yakima looked up from the box to see the driver hip around in the high seat and extend a cocked Remington revolver at him, baring his large, yellow teeth like a snarling, rabid cur.

The Remington roared.

The wagon was bouncing around too much for accurate shooting. The bullet screeched over Yakima's head to bury itself in the tailgate. The man glanced forward, keeping one eye on the trail, then fired again... and again.

Both bullets thumped loudly into the bed of the wagon within inches of where Yakima crouched. He raked his own Colt from its holster and, bracing himself with his free hand against the side of the wagon box, lined up the Colt's sights on the driver's head.

The man turned again toward Yakima, intending to fire another round. He hesitated when he saw the half-breed's six-shooter aimed at his head. He opened his mouth to scream but didn't get a sound out before a quarter-sized hole was blown into his forehead, just above the bridge of his nose. He jerked back and disappeared.

The wagon lurched violently right, then left.

Then right again.

Ah, shit.

The only problem with Yakima's tactic was that now the wagon was a runaway on one hell of a curving trail between thick chaparral and unforgiving boulders.

The cold thought had just buffeted across his brain when the wagon lurched again to the right, then the left.

Back to the right again, ricocheting off something hard.

It caromed wildly back across the trail before again smashing into something unyielding—probably a boulder—on the trail's left side. That front corner leaped up as Yakima heard the wagon breaking free of the team, and the mules brayed raucously.

For what seemed a long time but was likely only a second or two, he was aware of nothing but a sense of flying through air, then rolling in dust and over rocks and cactus patches. The world was a gray-brown blur swirling around him. He saw his Colt fly out of his hand. His right knee came up to smash his left cheek.

He yowled and grunted and cursed through gritted teeth.

Vaguely, he heard the thunder of the wagon rolling wildly on down the trail, bouncing off rocks and being turned to little more than kindling.

Beneath a shrill ringing in his ears, there was only silence.

He lay still. Mercifully still. He felt his cheek pressed against the ground.

Hooves thumped. He could feel the reverberations in the ground beneath him. When the hooves stopped, he rolled onto his back with a ragged groan to see Jake Salko staring down at him, eyes wide beneath his hat brim, from which clay-colored dust dripped.

Salko shook his head and grinned, eyes flashing. "Well, you're a crazy sonofabitch, I'll give you that!"

Yakima spat dirt from his mouth, cleared his throat. "I thought… you were dead."

Salko reached into the breast pocket of his pinstriped shirt, near a rawhide suspender, and withdrew a smashed, gold-washed pocket watch. "The bullet glanced off my old turnip. Can you beat that?"

Yakima shook his head. "Nope… don't reckon… I can."

Salko laughed.

Yakima spat dirt to one side. Blood was mixed with his spit. "The… robbers…?"

"All dead. They killed two of my men, wounded four more. They likely would have taken us all if you hadn't warned us. I'm much obliged, Henry. I know Kosgrove will be, too." Salko frowned down at him with obligatory concern. "How you doin'?"

"I, uh… I don't, uh… reckon I know… for sure."

"Ah, hell, you're fit as a fiddle!" Salko laughed again, then galloped on up the trail to where the wagon likely lay like a boxful of strewn matchsticks, the strongbox nestled inside the rubble.

More hoof thuds sounded. "Yakima!"

Emma galloped out of the chaparral. She'd lost her hat, and she was coated in dust. She reined the buckskin to a skidding halt and leaped out of the saddle.

"Yakima!"

"Ah, shit."

She ran over and dropped to a knee beside him. She stared down at him, pressing her hands to his face. "Are you all right? Please tell me you're not dead."

"Do I look dead?"

"How do you feel, you idiot?"

With a grunt, Yakima sat up, trying to blink away the fog in his brain. A hundred aches and pains were awakening in him, adding to the multitude that had plagued him since his bushwhacking and tumble into the canyon. "I don't know. Not so good, but… I'm still kickin', I reckon…"

"I thought you were dead for sure!"

Emma kissed him, wrapped her arms around his neck, and hugged him. He'd be damned if, in spite of everything, she didn't feel good in his arms. Warm and supple and... good.

Damn her!

More hoof thuds.

When the thuds grew louder and then died, Yakima looked up to see the Rio Grande Kid scowling down at him. The Kid shook his head, brushed a sheepish fist across his mouth, and looked away. "No, sir. Never did see a fella with a more complicated life."

The Kid shook his head again, touched spurs to his bay's flanks, and galloped away.

A Look At: Chiricahua Blues:
A Yakima Henry Western

The town marshal of Apache Springs, Arizona Territory,
Yakima Henry, has his hands full. Not only has the iron
horse arrived in a storm of frenzied hoopla, bringing more
crime along with it to the boomtown Apache Springs, but
Emma Kosgrove's secret canyon has been discovered.

One of the two young Southern brothers who stumbled into the canyon is dead, but it's unclear how he died
or who killed him. The other brother was so traumatized
by whatever happened to the other brother that he can't
speak, just walks around in a daze, muttering the single
word, "Snake," over and over again...

Yakima's senior deputy, the Rio Grande Kid, has his
own hands full of more trouble than he thought possible
when he pinned the star on his shirt. Yakima sends "the
Kid" to Tucson to fetch the murdering rapist, Darl Deakin,
and bring him by stagecoach to Apache Springs for trial.

AVAILABLE NOVEMBER 2021

ABOUT THE AUTHOR

Peter Brandvold grew up in the great state of North Dakota in the 1960's and '70s, when television westerns were as popular as shows about hoarders and shark tanks are now, and western paperbacks were as popular as Game of Thrones.

Brandvold watched every western series on television at the time. He grew up riding horses and herding cows on the farms of his grandfather and many friends who owned livestock.

Brandvold's imagination has always lived and will always live in the West. He is the author of over a hundred lightning-fast action westerns under his own name and his pen name, Frank Leslie.

Printed in Great Britain
by Amazon

24891026R00146